ꞮꞀ o

and the DEADHEADS

THE AVENGER

00073

To Harry
who gave the answer
– and Glory

First published in 1997 by
Andersen Press Limited

This edition published in 1998 by
Macdonald Young Books,
an imprint of Wayland Publishers
61 Western Road
Hove
BN3 1JD

Text © Roy Apps 1997

British Library Cataloguing in Publication Data is available.

ISBN 0 7500 2186 1

Phototypeset by Intype London Ltd
Printed and bound in Great Britain by
The Guernsey Press Co Ltd

Cover illustration © Paul Young 1997

THE AVENGER

Roy Apps

MACDONALD YOUNG BOOKS

Melvin
(**and the DEADHEADS**)

I

The wood crackles and spits excitedly in the large open fireplace of the old farmhouse. The four of them stare into the flames.

'We're safe enough. And we've still got the Virtual Reality encoder.'

'Suppose the police come sniffing around,' mutters Harry Summerskill.

'Do you really think those travellers are going to go to the police to report their buses missing?' says Angie.

'What about Perkins and the girl?'

'Oh come on, Harry, act your age! Who are the police going to believe, a respected television journalist and a local school teacher or a couple of kids?'

'That Perkins boy must know a lot by now,' mutters Harry.

'I told you he has power,' says Darius.

'How can he have? You've read the Black Book. The power is invested in us only,' insists Angie.

Darius speaks again. 'Whatever, there are four of us and only one of him. Governments, armies, criminal organisations the world over are waiting on the results of our experiments. No boy, empowered or not, is going to come between us and the wealth and the influence that is our rightful destiny.'

'Then before we continue, the boy must be put out of action,' suggests Angie. 'But Darius is right, the House does seem to have some sort of pull on him. We need to get him here.'

'How?' asks Harry. 'He's seen me and Darius – and you, Angie – in action. He won't trust any of us.'

Guy speaks for the first time. 'He'll trust me,' he says. 'And, after all, I know him better than any of you.' He pauses. 'He likes me.'

There is not the slightest flicker of any emotion in his pale, gaunt face.

1

'I want to do murder!' said Melvin.

Over the last couple of terms, Melvin Perkins had grown to like Mr Gibbons. This was handy because Melvin Perkins saw Mr Gibbons every day of the school year: Mr Gibbons was Melvin's form tutor.

However ... and it was a big however ...

Melvin just wished that he wouldn't *drone* on so.

This afternoon was typical.

'Poor Laws ... Corn Laws ...' Melvin heard Mr Gibbons saying. What was he wittering on about?

As usual, Melvin's mind began to drift idly. He wondered if the Gibbon – for this was the name by which he was generally known to everyone in 8GG – could get into the Guinness Book of Records for the World's Longest Ever Drone. After much deliberation, he decided it was doubtful: no one would be able to stay awake long enough to *time* the drone.

Melvin touched his forehead. It was hot and sweaty. So were the palms of his hands. The back of his shirt clung to him like a wet sponge, but his mouth was as dry as a cream cracker. All around him faces glistened with perspiration, eyes glazed over with torpor.

Kayleigh Foster's eyes weren't glazed over with

torpor, though, he noticed. They were gazing at him. Her face had a strange sort of twisted-up expression, as if she'd eaten something particularly disagreeable for lunch. This was what Kayleigh thought of as her sexiest smile. Melvin quickly averted his eyes across the classroom to the high windows that looked out over the front of the school. They were new. None of them was open more than a few centimetres. They had special bolts fitted to stop them opening more than that. No wonder it was so hot.

Melvin remembered the day that they had been installed. 'These bolts have been fitted for safety reasons.' Esther (Mr Ranson B Ed: Head Teacher) had explained. 'To prevent foolish children from jumping out the windows.'

'Safety? Safety?' Melvin had said to his friend Pravi Patel. 'Purr-lees! Our classroom's on the ground floor!'

'Esther is not a stupid man,' Pravi had reasoned.

'You could have fooled me,' Melvin had retorted.

'You see, over the years, he's probably seen hundreds of Sir Norman Burke Middle School pupils leaping out of the windows when faced by the prospect of another half an hour of the Gibbon droning on at them,' Pravi had explained.

Melvin looked beyond the bolts to the view outside. The caretaker was giving the lawn its first cut of the year with his new turbo-charged ride-on lawn mower. How Melvin wished he could be out there on a day like this. He'd get on his bike and pedal out of town up to Hogman's Thorn House to see his friend Arnold Thomas.

'Melvin?'

Melvin snapped out of his reverie. 'Yes, sir?'

'I was asking you, Melvin, to recap briefly on what I've been talking about, for the benefit of those amongst us who have only just woken up.'

'Yes, sir.' Melvin racked his brain. What had the Gibbon been saying? He nudged Pravi in the seat next to him. Pravi jumped, then blinked hesitantly at Melvin as if he were trying to work out exactly where he was. Pravi hadn't been listening to the Gibbon, either.

Outside, the caretaker was having trouble with his turbo-charged ride-on lawn mower, which kept trying to veer off the lawn and crash into teachers' cars. Of course, now he remembered! Melvin suddenly knew what it was that the Gibbon had been droning on about.

'Lawns, sir,' said Melvin. 'Umm ... poor lawns and corn ...'

Melvin heard the sound of sniggering behind him. If it hadn't been for the fact that his neck was already warm enough to fry an egg on, he would have been getting hot under the collar.

'Would you care to expand on that, Melvin?' enquired the Gibbon, in the tone of a sadist throwing a drowning man a concrete lifebuoy.

Melvin clutched desperately at straws – or rather

at corn – but the only thing he could think of saying was, 'Ummm . . .'

An arm shot up jabbing the air excitedly, as if some invisible force was pulling it towards the ceiling. It was Cassandra Washbone's arm.

'Perhaps what Melvin means is that corn isn't very good for lawns. Makes poor lawns. Sir.' A typical thing for a class P.W.S.T. (Person What Spells Trouble) to say and Cassandra was still 8GG's P.W.S.T.

It seemed to Melvin as if everyone was falling off their seats with laughing. For the second time that afternoon, he found himself cursing Esther's far-sightedness in installing classroom windows you couldn't jump out of.

You traitor, thought Melvin. You mean, cold-hearted traitor!

'Hmm . . .' the Gibbon said dreamily, as if he had his mind on other things – like *now where did I leave my thumb rack?* 'Perhaps you could explain, Melvin, why I should be discussing the finer points of lawn care during a History lesson?'

Melvin couldn't. But then teachers prattled on about all sort of weird things during lessons. He remembered the time the Leek (Mr Rhys-Williams: Expressive Arts) had spent half a lesson telling them a joke featuring a string vest, a cheese straw and a bottle of Fairy Liquid. Then there was the occasion when Spenda (Miss Penny: Geography and Personal and Social Education) had spent a whole lesson and half a break time asking the class why they thought her cat Twinkie had gone missing. (Probably couldn't stand her bad breath, Melvin had reckoned.)

Out of the corner of his eye, Melvin could still see the caretaker trying to control his turbo-charged, ride-on lawn mower. He was having all the success of a three-year-old trying to handle a dodgem car.

'Sir, the caretaker's having trouble with his mower – and he's near the teachers' cars. I think someone should tell Mr Ranson – '

'Melvin, the school caretaker's horticultural skills are no concern of yours – or mine, for that matter. Now would somebody care to put Melvin out of his misery and explain what I've been talking about?' the Gibbon asked.

'Sir, sir, ME, SIR!' Cassandra Washbone's voice. 'I'll put him out of his misery!'

You traitor, thought Melvin, once again. You mean, cold-hearted traitor!

'Go on, Cassandra,' said the Gibbon.

'You were talking about the nineteenth century Corn Laws and Poor Laws, sir, and how they affected the villages around Smallham,' gushed Cassandra. And she tossed her long dark hair back from her face as she said it.

How come she didn't look at all hot or bothered or parched, thought Melvin. Probably because she was a cold-blooded animal. He shot her a cold stare

11

and was sure she gave him half a triumphant wink in return.

'Indeed I was, Cassandra,' agreed the Gibbon. 'Because each and every one of you – and that includes you, Melvin – will be producing a written project on "Smallham in the Past", to be handed in to me during the first week of next term.'

Damien Higgins raised a weary hand. 'Sir, we break up next week. How can we finish the project in four days?'

'You can't, Damien,' replied the Gibbon with an unmistakable note of relish in his voice. 'But you can finish the project in four days plus two and a half weeks.'

'Sir!' A chorus of protest filled the dank air.

'That's right,' the Gibbon continued, with a sly twinkle in his eye. 'The "Smallham in the Past" project is something for you to do during the Easter holidays. Think of it as an end of term present from me, to stop you all getting bored. Besides, you've got an extra two days off while we poor members of staff sweat it out on In-Service Training. It'll help me concentrate on my studies to know that you are all going to be usefully employed in academic endeavours. You can make a start for tonight's homework.'

Thirty heartfelt groans replaced the chorus of protest. But the Gibbon didn't hear them. This was hardly surprising, as he had a specially modified brain that was biochemically incapable of processing messages of complaint, especially from Year 8 pupils.

'So,' said the Gibbon, beaming from ear to ear, 'can I have your chosen topics, please?' The Gibbon's eyes scanned the classroom for his first victim. 'Cassandra?'

' "Television in Victorian Smallham",' said Cassandra, brightly. It was the classic reply of a P.W.S.T.

Twenty-nine voices roared with laughter. The Gibbon silenced all of them with one steely look. 'The Victorians didn't have television, Cassandra.'

Out of the corner of his eye, Melvin saw Cassandra's jaw drop, as if she was incapable of comprehending such an extraordinary piece of information. But she wasn't stupid, Melvin knew – certainly not that stupid. She was clever. Indeed, sometimes she was too clever for her own good.

'As well you know,' added the Gibbon, through clenched teeth.

'If they didn't have telly, what did they *do*, sir?' asked Cassandra.

Melvin saw a look of horror cross Cassandra's face as, too late, she realised that she had walked straight into a trap.

'That's for you to find out, isn't it, Cassandra?' the Gibbon beamed. 'I'll put you down for "Pastimes and Entertainment in Victorian Smallham".'

Cassandra sank slowly down the back of her chair – the last act of a drowning woman. She knew she had only herself to blame.

'Melvin?' enquired the Gibbon. 'Can I have your topic, please? And don't even think about suggesting "Computer Games in Saxon Smallham".'

Melvin knew exactly what he was going to suggest and it wasn't "Computer Games in Saxon Smallham". For the first time that afternoon, the stuffy classroom didn't bother him. He was excited. He couldn't wait to start his local history project.

'I want to do murder!' said Melvin.

'Murder?'

'Murder in Smallham.'

The Gibbon sighed. 'Shall we call it "Crime and Punishment Over the Years" instead, Melvin?'

'Okay,' said Melvin, with a shrug. He didn't really care what the Gibbon called it. *He* knew what he was going to do his project on. He knew exactly which Smallham murder he was going to investigate for his project. It was a murder he was not just going to investigate, but to avenge.

'Pravikumar, what about you?'

Pravi's reply sounded like a grudging grunt of acceptance. In fact, it was a snore.

'Pravi?' The Gibbon's tone had become suspicious. He began to walk down from the front of the classroom towards Pravi. 'How about "A Short History of Smallham Schools"?'

Melvin nudged his friend. Pravi snored some more. Was nothing going to wake him? The Gibbon was only two metres from his desk.

14

Suddenly, from outside, there came the sound of an almighty crash. Metal was tearing on metal.

Thirty members of 8GG – including Pravi – shot to their feet, just in time to see the caretaker bury his turbo-charged ride-on lawn mower into the front nearside wing of the Gibbon's Vauxhall Astra.

'I did try to warn you, sir – ' began Melvin.

But the Gibbon, his face as pink as a map of the nineteenth century British Empire, had already rushed from the room.

'Huh?' The noise had woken Pravi with a start. 'Coming, Mum,' he shouted.

Then he looked around, astonished to find himself, not in his bed at the start of another day, but in his tutor group room at the end of a History lesson.

II

The windows in the hotel bedroom are shut fast, but even so are unable to deaden completely the roar of the London traffic outside.

Two of them sit in uncomfortable armchairs. Opposite them sits the man they have come to see. He picks his nose for a few seconds. He examines the clean contours of his fingernails. Only then does he speak.

'What you have described would, of course, have considerable value to a range of people with whom I have contact – governments, secret service organisations, even certain large multi-national companies. We are talking seven figures here, easily. I shall of course require a certain percentage. You may have the merchandise, but I have the contacts.'

'What percentage?' asks the woman, cagily.

'Before we proceed any further with negotiations, I need to see evidence that what you claim you can do actually works.'

'We have set up a demonstration. You will be able to see the various stages of deadheading at work on a number of . . . subjects,' replies the woman.

The man they have come to see cleans his ear with his little finger. 'Good,' he says at last. 'I think we are in business.'

He does not shake hands with them.

As they sit in the throbbing South London traffic on their way home, the man turns to his colleague. 'Do you really think he'll be interested in something so . . . so devastating, so final *as deadheading?'*

'For goodness' sake, Darius, get a life,' sneers the woman. 'He used to be at the Ministry of Defence. He's sold landmines, knowing they could maim inno-cent kids. He's sold guns to terrorists and tanks to dictators. He's interested in deadheading all right.'

'Even the ultimate stage, Angie?'

'Even the ultimate stage.'

'Then all we can do now is to pray that Guy can deliver us the subjects at the appointed place, at the appointed time.'

Angie's face sets hard. 'And, more importantly, to pray that he can deliver us the Perkins boy.'

2

'Hey, be careful, pal, there are some really weird people out there.'

As Melvin waited on the corner of the High Street for the last straggling groups of Sir Norman Burke students to make their way into the various news-agents', he wondered what on earth it was that drove someone to murder someone else. By the time the coast was clear and he turned into the side street that led to Cassandra Washbone's house, he thought he knew the answer.

He rang the bell on the bright red front door and heard Cassandra bounding down the stairs.

The door opened and she peeked round.

'You sure no one saw you coming up here?' she whispered furtively.

'The hit squad's coming in the back door, *traitor*,' snapped Melvin. 'Now let me in.'

He followed Cas through to the kitchen. Some-thing small, grey and hairy clawed at his trouser leg.

'Down, Scratch!' commanded Cas. 'Down, boy!'

Cas's dog growled grumpily, then crawled back to his basket.

'That's odd,' said Cas. 'He's not usually like that with you. He usually only goes for window cleaners and armed robbers.'

'Perhaps,' replied Melvin acidly, 'he senses that

I've come here with evil intent.'

'Have you?'

'Yes,' said Melvin, firmly.

'What kind of evil intent?' asked Cas innocently.

'I'm going to thump you with my local history project book until your head is as flat as a thin crust pizza,' replied Melvin with as much evil intent as he could muster.

'Oh right,' said Cas, airily. 'If you want to eat it when you've done with it, you'll find the parmesan cheese in the cupboard. In the meantime, have a drink.' She tossed Melvin a can of Coke.

'You think I'm joking, don't you?' said Melvin, ever the one to state the blindingly obvious.

'Put it this way,' said Cas. 'I don't think you're the sort of boy who hits girls.'

Actually, this wasn't absolutely true – Melvin regularly gave his little sister Ellie a thump.

'At least,' added Cas, looking down at her feet. 'I don't think you're the sort of boy who hits girls who wear size eight Cats.'

This *was* absolutely true.

'I want to know why you think it's so cool to make me look a prize dork in class.'

'You should've been paying attention to the Gibbon.'

'And you should've been showing some sort of solidarity!' exclaimed Melvin, exasperatedly. 'You're a traitor, Cassandra Washbone!'

'How so?'

19

'How so?' repeated Melvin. 'I mean . . . I thought we were . . .' He struggled for words. Then gave up, not daring to say what he really wanted to say – '*I thought we were friends.*'

Cas sat down at the kitchen table opposite Melvin. She took a swig of Coke, then leant across the table towards Melvin.

'Melv, I can't afford to let anyone know . . .'

'Know what?'

'That you come round here drinking our Coke.'

'Why?' muttered Melvin. 'Bad for your image, is it?'

'Yes . . . there is that, of course,' responded Cas, thoughtfully. 'You know what I mean, Melv. You are, how shall I put it . . . ?' She took another swig of Coke, then looked into Melvin's face with her round, dark eyes. 'Mad, bad and dangerous to know.'

'You mean the deadheaders?' said Melvin, quietly.

'Uh-huh. Nothing personal, Melv. It's just that there's a group of people with the means to turn us all into zombies and because you're somehow the key to it all, they're trying to do nasty things to you. They've tried kidnapping you, setting Rottweilers onto you and deadheading you. Goodness knows what'll be next.'

Melvin swallowed hard. 'You sure know how to make a guy feel good,' he sighed. 'Anyway, you can stop making me look a dork at school.'

Cas shook her head. 'You can't trust anyone, Melv.' She aimed her empty Coke can at the bin, threw and missed.

'You're an idiot, going up there again.'

'Going up where?' asked Melvin, innocently.

'Oh, come on, Melv,' snorted Cas. 'There's only one reason you started leaping up and down like a baby on a bouncy castle at the thought of doing a History project – you're going to write all about the murder of your Victorian ghost friend.'

'Want to come?' asked Melvin.

Cas ignored Melvin's question. She was suddenly very serious. 'Melv, keep clear of Hogman's Thorn. History project or no History project. If the dead-headers catch you snooping around again . . .'

'Cas, the last time they tried anything was months ago; back before Christmas.'

'Do you really think they've given up, just because we messed it up for them last time?'

'Yeah,' said Melvin, unconvincingly. He was a terrible liar. 'Anyway, I must get home.'

At the front door, Cas grabbed Melvin's arm. 'Just let me make sure there's no one about before you go.'

'Who do you think might be there? One of the deadheaders?'

'No, Kayleigh Foster.'

'Kayleigh?'

'Yes. She'd murder me if she knew you'd been round here.'

'Why?'

'She fancies you, doesn't she?'

'Does she?'

21

'Like crazy. Didn't you know?'

'No.'

'Honestly, Melv, you don't notice anything, do you?'

Cas peered gingerly round the front door.

'Right! The coast is clear. Off you go.' She grabbed his arm as he stepped out. 'And hey, be careful, pal, there are some really weird people out there. And they're after you. And you're just the sort of dork not to see them coming.'

Melvin kicked open the front gate. He wished he understood girls. Kayleigh Foster, fancying him? He shut his eyes to try and banish the dreadful thought from his mind. Kayleigh Foster was even taller than the Gibbon. Other girls in 8GG read *Teen Dreams* and *Top Girl* magazine, Kayleigh read *Combat Soldier*. Other girls in 8GG carried lipstick in their bags, Kayleigh carried a baseball bat in hers.

Perhaps it was all one of Cas's famous wind-ups. No, he remembered the peculiar smile on Kayleigh's face when he had caught her staring at him in class. He sighed. How he wished he understood girls. Not just Kayleigh, but Cas. Sometimes she seemed like the only person he could say things to, but other times she was still a P.W.S.T.

He went into hiding in his room and didn't come out until tea time.

'More ravioli, anyone?' asked Mrs Perkins, more in hope than expectation.

Three heads shook.

'Hannah, you've not had any,' said Mrs Perkins, gently.

'I can't eat pasta, Mum,' explained Melvin's older sister.

'You did last week.'

'I was a vegan then.'

'What are you this week then, dear?'

'A fruitarian,' replied Hannah.

Melvin groaned. He wished he understood his older sister. She changed diets faster than Man United changed their away kit.

'Some more for you, Ellie?'

'Don't like spinach,' said Melvin's younger sister.

'There isn't any spinach in it,' replied Mrs Perkins.

'There is,' insisted Ellie.

'I made it, Ellie, and there is no spinach in it.' Mrs Perkins was reasonableness itself.

'Well I can taste it,' insisted Ellie.

Melvin groaned again. He wished he understood his younger sister.

'Some more for you, Melvin?'

'No thanks, Mum.'

Mrs Perkins smiled wistfully at her son. 'Do you remember when you were little, you used to call it messy-oli?'

'No,' lied Melvin. Of course he remembered. He remembered his dad chortling with laughter every time he'd said messy-oli.

'I thought we might all go out for a family night

on Friday,' Melvin's mum prattled on, seemingly unmoved by her family's total rejection of her ravioli. 'Go and see a film or something. There's the new Disney on in Worthing.' She sounded unbearably bright.

'Mum, please, I'm almost sixteen,' said Hannah.

'I'm staying at Tamara's house on Friday,' said Ellie.

'Oh well, just a thought!' trilled Mrs Perkins.

Melvin washed up his plate and went back upstairs to his room. He wished he understood his mum. How could she be so cheerful – at this time of the year! On Saturday it would be March 21st: six years to the day since his dad had left for work as usual and never returned. He wished he understood his dad. Why had he gone off like that? What had made him change? Melvin wondered if his dad still thought about him, like he did him, every day of the week?

Kayleigh, Cas, Hannah, Ellie, his mum, his dad – he didn't understand any of them. Was there nobody he knew who was sensible, straightforward, someone with whom you knew where you were? Someone you could talk to?

A couple of minutes later, Melvin was pedalling out of town and up the steep hill towards Hogman's Thorn.

Yes, of course there was someone he could talk to.

III

The wood crackles and spits excitedly in the large open fireplace of the old farmhouse.

The four of them stare into the flames. What pictures do they see there? Pictures of their futures – as some of the richest, most powerful people on earth?

They know their time has come. Angie and Darius have already told the other two about their visit to London.

'Is the subliminal imaging apparatus in good order?' Angie asks.

Harry Summerskill nods. 'It worked a treat on Guy's caretaker fellow.'

'Indeed,' agrees Guy. 'The poor fellow's mind was so addled he managed to write off three cars in the staff car park this afternoon. He was dismissed instantly – as was the plan. Our man, safely dead-headed by Darius, should fill the vacant post in a couple of days. That will give us added security in the coming weeks, should anything go wrong.'

'Nothing will go wrong,' says Angie, coldly. 'And, Guy, it is unnecessarily sentimental to refer to the ex-caretaker as a "poor fellow". His sacrifice was necessary in our pursuit of a successful outcome to *our magnificent project.'*

'Of course, Angie,' concurs Guy.

'The equipment for my part of the proceedings has already been delivered,' Angie reminds them. 'So, Guy, are our "volunteers" ready and willing?'

'Yes.'

'And your man's game?'

'I'm meeting him at the House in half an hour.'

'And have you worked out firm details for dealing with the boy?'

'It's not going to be easy.'

'He knows you. Why can't you just bring him here?'

'Simply because of that – he knows me! He'll blab afterwards.'

Not a glimmer of emotion crosses Darius's face. 'It never occurred to me that there would be any "afterwards" for him. Surely he has to be dealt with permanently?'

There is a murmur of agreement from Harry.

And Angie, as if to make sure that Guy understands the meaning of the word 'permanent', runs a long varnished fingernail across her neck.

'In that case,' says Guy, slowly, 'there is a very good way of luring him here. The whole of his class are engaged on a History project – '

'Spare us the details, Guy,' mutters Darius. 'Just bring us the boy.'

3

'Tables filled with row upon row of silver carving knives and skewers . . .'

The sign was new. Smart black lettering on white wood: HOGMAN'S THORN HOUSE: THE CON-FERENCE CENTRE.

Melvin wheeled his bike into the woods that bordered the grounds of Hogman's Thorn House. He sat down and leant back against the large oak tree that overhung the wall, trying to get his breath. HOGMAN'S THORN HOUSE: THE CONFER-ENCE CENTRE meant only one thing to Melvin: the deadheaders were back. With an involuntary shiver, he wondered just what kind of deadheading programme they were planning this time.

Melvin had not been back to Hogman's Thorn since the business with the travellers. There had been Christmas, then the usual winter 'flu, then snow and ice all but cutting off Hogman's Thorn from Smallham and the rest of the world.

Melvin took his rope out of the bike panniers, clambered up the tree and crawled out along the branch that fanned out over the garden. He knotted the rope onto the branch, then swung down it into the garden.

Something didn't feel quite right and it was a moment or two before he realised what it was:

although he knew what he was doing was dangerous, *he didn't feel at all scared*. In a way, he wished he did, for then he would have been back on his bike and away before you could say dead-head. As it was, he was standing in the fading light of the garden of Hogman's Thorn House.

One or two forsythia bushes were blazing their bright yellow flowers, but apart from that, the trees and shrubs were bare and Melvin could actually see the house.

'A happy yuletide and a most prosperous new year to you, Perkins.'

Melvin spun round and saw the familiar figure of Arnold Thomas. Nothing about the Victorian delinquent ghost had altered one bit. His filthy hair was as much a ginger mophead as it had ever been: it had grown no longer, nor had it been cut short. He was still scruffy. His trousers were still ripped right up to the knee, his shirt was still missing a collar, the same shirt he had been wearing when Melvin had first seen him the previous summer. He was, in every way, reassuringly unchanged.

'Hi, Arnold. Er . . . are you keeping well?'

'Am I keeping well?' Arnold snorted. 'Perkins, I am a ghost. I am not at all well. I am *dead.*'

No, in every way, Arnold was reassuringly unchanged. He was even as grumpy as ever.

'Yes . . . of course,' mumbled Melvin.

'Not that I would have blamed you for never setting foot in this abominable place again.' Arnold

28

nodded in the direction of the house, from where downstairs, lights glowed in the twilight.

'They're back, aren't they?'

'Yes, they're back, Perkins. The same four faces as before. There's a new man in tonight though. Whispering darkly with the one they call Guy.'

Guy. The one I've never seen, thought Melvin. He looked over towards the house, but he could see no sign of any life behind the dimly-lit windows.

'There aren't any killer dogs, or thugs armed with sticks about?'

Arnold shook his head.

'What have they got in there?' asked Melvin

'Downstairs: tables, chairs . . .' replied Arnold. He paused. If it hadn't been for the fact that he knew he was a ghost, Melvin would have sworn he saw Arnold shiver. 'Upstairs they have a darkened chamber containing tables filled with row upon row of silver carving knives and skewers.'

Melvin recalled how Arnold had mistaken a gym for a torture chamber.

'You're sure it's not just a kitchen?'

'If a kitchen it is,' replied Arnold sharply, 'then I'll wager my breeches that their intent isn't merely to boil up a few mutton chops.'

Arnold was right. Harry Summerskill, Darius O'Fee, Angie Allbright and the fourth one called Guy weren't going to build anything in Hogman's Thorn House, unless it could be used in some sort of deadheading process.

29

'There is a bed in this chamber,' Arnold added.

'A bed?' To Melvin, who knew that the deadheaders were at their most dangerous when their intended victims were relaxed, sleepy even, this was the most sinister fact of the lot.

'What are you going to do this time, Perkins?'

'Make connections,' said Melvin. 'Remember what you told me after the business with the travellers? That the deadheaders could *sense* you? That you and they were connected in some way? Find the connections, you said. That's what I'm going to do.'

'I'm glad to hear it, old man. Where do you intend to start?'

'I thought maybe I could get a look at your Birth Certificate – and your Death Certificate.'

'My ma never bothered with a Birth Certificate for any of us. And my Death Certificate was signed by a quack doctor as death from pneumonia. You'll find nothing there. *I* can tell you all you need to know about my murder. I remember it very well indeed.'

'Maybe, Arnold, but you see, I have to "consult contemporary sources".'

'Beg pardon?'

'For my History project.'

'Beg pardon again?' Arnold's pale face was completely blank.

'I'm investigating your murder for my History project. For school.'

'I don't want to be a *project*,' said Arnold, sulkily.

'Tough cookie. If you want me to avenge your murder you're going to have to be a History project. Now, I need to know the date of your birth and the date you were murdered.'

Arnold spoke grudgingly. 'My ma always told me I was born on either the thirteenth or fourteenth of June eighteen sixty-nine. She was never easy with dates. As to my murder, that was the twenty-first of March, eighteen eighty.

Melvin swallowed hard. 'Are you sure?'

'Of course I'm sure. Listen, Perkins, when you are living there's one date you never forget – and that's your birthday. When you're like me, there are only two dates you never forget, your birth date and the day you were murdered.'

'When you're like me,' said Melvin, 'there are two dates you remember. Your birthday and the day your dad left and never came back.'

'Ah yes, your pa,' said Arnold.

'The date my dad left,' Melvin said quietly, 'was the twenty-first of March. It's anniversary time – for us both.'

'Is it? I watch the seasons pass, that is all.'

'But you must know what has happened here since the day you were murdered?' Melvin asked.

Arnold shrugged. 'The Master died. The Mistress died. Their son took over the school. The thrashings, the beatings, went on. The son had a daughter; she closed the school. But she was an evil old witch.

Her grandchildren were all born here. Then it was empty until . . . well you know the rest.'

'Is that it?' exclaimed Melvin.

'What more do you want?'

'Dates!' said Melvin, with exasperation. 'I'll need to draw a time line for my project.'

'Fiddle-me-ray,' snorted Arnold. 'Time? Dates? What are such things to a ghost? My life is an eternal one. Seasons come and go like the fluttering of an eyelid.'

Melvin sighed. 'There is one thing you might be able to help with, Arnold,' he said suddenly. 'Can you tell me what you and your mates used to get up to for amusement?'

'Is this for your History project too, Perkins.'

'No . . . no,' said Melvin, a little unsteadily.

'Swear on your grandmother's grave?'

'Er . . . yes,' said Melvin.

'I wasn't above a little bit of smatter-hauling,' whispered Arnold.

'A little bit of what?'

'Stealing handkerchiefs. Usually from gents awaiting the London train – '

'Arnold, I'm not interested in your criminal activities. I want to know about games . . . sport . . .'

'Smatter-hauling was our sport. Don't mistake me, Perkins, we were merry enough. We told each other stories about Black Jack Bonegrinder who sliced ladies' fingers off with his penknife to get their rings, Half-Hung Smith who stepped from the scaffold alive and Earl Ferrers who was hanged by a silk scarf because he was a Lord. And we sang songs that would make the likes of you blush. Do you reckon you'd like to hear one?'

Melvin grabbed a scrap of paper from his pocket – it was a piece of headed notepaper from school informing all pupils, or rather their parents, of the forthcoming In-Service Training days for teachers – and scribbled furiously. The song that Arnold sang did make Melvin blush. He'd never realised the Victorians knew about such things.

By the time Melvin had inched his way back up the rope to the branch, it was growing dark. The lights in the house still glowed, but there was no other sign of life.

Melvin dropped quietly down into the under-growth on the other side of the garden wall. Although he had felt curiously safe and un-frightened talking with Arnold just fifty metres or so from two deadheaders, he was relieved to be out of the grounds – the grounds that seemed to hold so much evil power.

He bent down to pick up his bike.

And felt a hand grab his shoulder.

So surprised was Melvin, that he let out a sudden involuntary scream. The hand – black leather-gloved – immediately slapped itself over his mouth. Melvin staggered to get up, broke free, but caught his shin on his bike pedal and fell heavily to the ground.

Scared, shocked and helpless, he looked up and saw standing over him a figure clothed, from knee-length jackboots to balaclava, entirely in black.

The other black leather-gloved hand – the one that had not grabbed Melvin – was held menacingly aloft. Its fingers gripped a large baseball bat and its fearful-looking owner looked ready to swing it.

IV

The one called Guy flings open the double doors with a flourish.

His colleague casts an appreciative eye around the room. He runs his hand over the huge teak-effect table in the middle of the room, then over the circle of leather chairs clustered around it.

'Splendid,' he says.

'There are overhead projectors, video playback facilities – all the usual conference centre hardware,' explains Guy. 'And the lecturers are all first class.' His face spreads into a smile. 'You can be sure that once you've been on a Hogman's Thorn training course, you'll never be quite the same again.'

'You've done an excellent job in setting this up for us, Guy, an excellent job,' smiles his colleague.

4

'Don't worry, Melv, I won't let you out of my sight . . . !'

Melvin flinched and instinctively covered his head with his hand.

The figure was muttering something incoherently.

Melvin felt the black leather glove grip his shoulder again. The figure's face was now close to his and for the first time he saw the large dark eyes.

'No! *You* . . . ?'

The figure mumbled some more.

'Take that stupid hat off, Washbone, and explain yourself,' said Melvin, wearily.

One black leather glove pulled at the balaclava. Cassandra Washbone shook her hair onto her shoulders and grinned sheepishly at Melvin. 'Hiya, kid,' she said.

'What are you doing up here?' spluttered Melvin.

'I came up to make sure you were okay . . . and not in any trouble.'

'Well, I'm not.' Melvin rubbed his ankle. 'At least, I wasn't until you jumped me in the bushes.'

'I didn't jump you.'

'I'm quite capable of looking after myself, anyway.'

'No, you're not!' retorted Cas. 'If I'd been one of the deadheaders, or Gormless the Guard or any other of their hired thugs, you'd be unconscious by now, Melvin Perkins.'

'Well I'm not,' grumbled Melvin, still rubbing his bruised shin. 'More to the point, how did you know I was up here?'

'Your sister told me.'

'How did she know?'

'She saw you riding off, stupid. She and I have come to an arrangement. She rings me if you look likely to do anything daft – like coming up to Hogman's Thorn alone and completely unprepared – and I'm going to put a good word in for her with my brother.'

'I thought she'd told him where to go?'

'She did, but now she wants to get back together with him. I think he still fancies her really – he should, she's dead pretty your sister – but he's still got Clarissa in tow.'

Melvin found himself struggling to keep up with the cast of characters in Cas's story.

'Who's Clarissa?'

'A girl at College. She's got orange and purple hair and she wears a bike chain round her ankle.'

'She wears a *what*?'

'It's a fashion statement. But I've already told Bunny he'd be better off looking in the direction of a girl who wears her clothes as a *passion* statement.'

Compared to Cas and Hannah's antics the devious workings of the deadheaders' minds were positively primitive, Melvin thought.

'And the outfit you're wearing,' said Melvin, 'is that meant to be a fashion statement – or the other?'

'This is a disguise,' said Cas, seriously. 'If I was to come up here, I certainly didn't want to be recognised by Darius O'Fee or Angie Allbright or any other of them. If you'd had any sense, you would have done the same.'

As they came out of the wood and onto the road, the sound of a car engine caught their ears. Suddenly, headlight beams picked out the road in front of Hogman's Thorn House. The one they called Guy and whoever it was who had been with him in the house, were leaving. Melvin and Cas pressed themselves against the high brick wall.

The car swung out of the drive and headed off down the hill towards Smallham.

'Did you get the number?' Cas asked.

'No.' Melvin felt his lips go dry. 'But it was new, it was red and it was a Mondeo.' He swallowed hard. 'I know someone who's got a new red Mondeo.'

'Who's that?' asked Cas.

'Esther.'

Cas nodded; her face showed no sign of surprise. 'Melv, over the last week or so, I've been thinking: what's been the one constant factor in the three deadheading attempts so far – apart from you?'

Melvin thought; shrugged; shook his head.

'Sir Norman Burke Middle School. Or rather one person at Sir Norman Burke Middle School. It was the school hall where the subliminal imaging took

38

place. Who was responsible for booking the dead-headers the hall?'

'Esther,' said Melvin.

'It was the school that was used as a recruitment centre for Darius O'Fee's Genius Academy,' Cas went on. 'Who was the world's greatest supporter of the Genius Academy?'

'Esther.'

'And it was at school where you and I narrowly missed being abducted by a bogus police officer. Who called the cops?'

Melvin nodded. 'Esther.'

'Esther, Esther, Esther,' echoed Cas.

Melvin shuddered. 'Why didn't you tell me before?' he stuttered.

'I didn't want to worry you.'

'You're so kind.'

'Now you know why I'm rude to you at school,' Cas said. 'I don't want Esther connecting me with you in any way. I've got to watch my own back. Like I said, it's nothing personal.'

'You think Esther's been deadheaded?' asked Melvin.

'Don't you?'

They walked down the hill into Smallham in silence. Then Melvin suddenly took the scrap of paper from his pocket and gave it to Cas.

'For your local history project,' he said. 'All good stuff about Victorian pastimes and that. Straight from the horse's mouth – not that Arnold would thank me for calling him a horse.'

'Thanks,' said Cas.

'That's all right,' said Melvin.

Cas opened her mouth to say something else, but stopped herself. Instead, she studied Melvin's notes in the fast-fading light.

'Melv, is that word what I think it is?' Cas was blushing.

Melvin took the scrap of paper back from Cas. 'Yep!' he said. 'There was an even ruder song, but I didn't write it down.'

'Shame,' said Cas.

Suddenly, the school logo at the top of the piece of paper caught Melvin's eye – or rather the name that was under it: Mr G. Ranson B Ed. Head Teacher.'

'Oh no,' groaned Melvin quietly. 'Look. G. Ranson. G for Guy. You've got it wrong. Esther's not been deadheaded. Far from it. Esther is a dead-header! He's Guy – the fourth man; the one neither of us has seen. The one who Arnold said was planning the next experiment in Hogman's Thorn House tonight! With skewers and carving knives!'

Melvin's mind raced. 'Do you think I should wag school?'

'Don't be daft,' said Cas. 'That's the first thing that will arouse Esther's suspicions. Don't worry, Melv, I won't let you out of my sight all the time we're at school.' She waved her baseball bat about her head.

'Where did you get that thing, Cas?'

'It belongs to – or rather it *did* belong to Kayleigh.'

'So what are you doing with it?'

'She wanted to do a swap with me. I thought it might come in very handy. I'm even more convinced now.'

'What did you give her in return?'

'Oh, didn't I say?' said Cas, uneasily.

'No, you didn't,' replied Melvin.

'Oh. I gave her your phone number.'

'What!'

'She said you were ex-directory. I thought it was a good deal, Melv. Who knows, one day, Kayleigh's baseball bat might even save your life.'

When he got in, Hannah was waiting for him. She had a broad smirk on her face.

'My, my, what a Romeo my little brother is. He's got one girlfriend bribing me to let her know his whereabouts and he's got another one who's been on the phone for him – three times!'

'Eh?' asked Melvin.

'Name of Kelly? Kylie? Kayleigh?'

Melvin groaned. Esther was after him to deadhead him, Kayleigh was after him to ... he didn't dare think what she was after him to do. He felt himself to be a hunted man. He went straight up to his room and shut the door.

That night he dreamt the happiest of dreams. His dad was back at home. They were having a barbecue in the back garden. Mum was laughing.

So real was his dream, that for a brief moment, when he woke up, he couldn't understand why his dad wasn't standing by his bed saying, 'Come on, Melvin, you'll be late for school, son.'

When he realised, he just turned over in his bed and wished he could go back to sleep – into *that* sleep with *that* dream – for ever. Only when the last warm and comforting images from the dream had finally drifted away from him, did Melvin open his eyes. He wished he'd had a nightmare, he really did. At least when you woke up from a nightmare, you were glad it was all over.

In the classroom, in the corridor, in the playground, in the dining hall, all next day at school Melvin made sure he was not alone. This was not a problem. Always within shouting distance was Cas; though for her, shouting distance was about two hundred metres. And always, within winking distance, was Kayleigh.

Not that Melvin saw anything of his Head Teacher all day, for just as vampires only rarely venture out during the hours of daylight, so Esther only rarely ventured out of his office during school hours.

'Right,' said the Gibbon, clapping his hands enthusiastically, 'how are these History projects shaping up?' His eagle eye scanned thirty wearisome faces. 'Cassandra?'

Cas proceeded to regale 8GG with the most gory details of the lives of Black Jack Bonegrinder and Half-Hanged Smith. The Gibbon could not fail but be impressed.

'Well done, Cas. Pravikumar?'

'I found a book in the school library about the history of our school, sir.'

'Go on, Pravi.'

Pravi took a deep breath and peered at his notes. 'Sir Norman Burke Middle School was named after Sir Norman Burke 1860 to 1925, the Principal of an institution for delinquent boys called Flogmore Hall – it's called Hogman's Thorn House now – where his father Mr Obadiah Burke 1835 to 1900 had also been the Master – '

Pravi came up for air. Melvin's mind swam. Why had he never thought to ask Arnold the name of his Master?

'The Burkes were well-known for their humane and caring educational philosophy in what was often a brutal age,' Pravi went on. 'Hundreds of boys who passed through their hands testified to the Burkes' kindness and generosity. They would often go without food so that the boys in their care were properly fed.'

Melvin could take no more.

'Pravi's got it all wrong,' he blurted out.

Pravi looked up from his notes in astonishment.

'I haven't, sir, it's all in this book.'

'Obviously it is,' agreed the Gibbon, 'and you

43

appear to have copied it out word for word.'

'But, sir, the Burkes were evil and cruel. They flogged the boys at their school. They even murdered one of them!'

Everyone in the class turned to stare at Melvin, much in the same way as you might turn to stare at a drunk in the street who starts shouting and cursing.

'What are your sources, Melvin? Where is your evidence?' asked the Gibbon.

The ghost of a Victorian delinquent, thought Melvin.

'Um ... er ...' said Melvin.

'What have we been learning in History all term?' sighed the Gibbon.

'State your sources, weigh up the evidence, sir,' said Cas, with a sly wink at Melvin.

'Thank you, Cassandra,' said the Gibbon.

'There's even a picture in this book,' said Pravi. 'You can see how happy everyone looks.'

Melvin looked at the picture. Three rows of cropped-haired boys, all dressed in roll-necked jumper and thick long shorts, stared out at him. They all had smiles on their faces ... Pravi was right, but the smiles were blank and distant. They looked like deadheads.

'How is your own project coming along, Melvin?' asked the Gibbon.

The bell rang for the end of school, sparing Melvin further embarrassment.

'Wait for it, 8GG,' yelled the Gibbon above the sudden din. He placed himself in front of the door while the mob moved back a little. Then he flung open the door and retreated behind his desk.

'Melvin!' he called. 'A word, please!'

The noise drifted away.

'Sit down, Melvin.'

Melvin perched on the end of a desk.

'So how is your History project shaping up?'

'I've got a bit stuck, sir,' Melvin admitted. 'I know the murder I want to write up.'

'Indeed? Anything to do with Flogmore Hall by any chance?'

Melvin nodded. 'I know it happened, sir!'

'How?'

'Somebody told me . . .'

The Gibbon frowned. 'You mean an elderly person who had the story passed down to them?'

A very elderly person, thought Melvin. 'Yes, sir.'

'But you haven't got any real evidence.'

Melvin shook his head.

The Gibbon thought for a moment. 'I might be able to help there. Old editions of *The Smallham Gazette*, that's what you need. You've got the date of this murder?'

'Twenty-first of March, eighteen eighty.'

'Good. Now, you can't get copies dating from the eighteen hundreds at the library, but they do keep them at the *Gazette* head office in Worthing. A mate of mine works there. I could give him a ring if you like, fix up for you to go over and see him?'

Melvin tried to think if there was a way of explaining to the Gibbon that this particular murder wouldn't be in the paper, for the simple reason that no one – apart from him and the victim – knew it was murder. He couldn't.

'Shall we say tomorrow, after school?' suggested the Gibbon.

'Yes, sir. Thank you, sir.'

Melvin saw a familiar head bob down behind the window. True to her word, Cas wasn't going to let him out of her sight while he was at school, particularly after school, when Esther was most likely to be on the prowl.

Melvin reached the school gates without encountering Esther. Out of the corner of his eye, he saw Cas pop up behind the bins outside the kitchens and then pop down again. He turned round and found himself facing Kayleigh.

'Hi, Melv!'

'Oh. Kayleigh.'

'I tried ringing you last night.'

'I know.'

'You were out.'

'I know,' said Melvin, but the sarcasm in his voice just seemed to wash over Kayleigh. He decided to try a more direct approach. 'I was up Hogman's Thorn woods,' he said airily, 'with Cas Washbone.'

Kayleigh's jaw dropped like a stone. 'The great, big, ugly – ' she yelled, using a word, which if she had been on the football field would have earned her an early bath.

'Anyway, I wouldn't be seen dead going out with you, you pathetic little skunk, Melvin Perkins,' she added. 'And when you see her, tell her I want my baseball bat back, or else I'll pull her gizzards out.'

'Right,' said Melvin.

Cas popped up behind the bins just in time to see Kayleigh stomping off up the road. Melvin beckoned her over.

'What was all that about?' she asked.

Melvin shrugged. 'Oh, you know, lovers' tiff,' he said.

Cas stuck her tongue out at him.

'Somehow I don't think she'll be ringing me tonight.'

'What did you say to her?'

'Oh, just a few well-chosen words,' grinned Melvin. 'I reckoned I was safe enough, seeing as how you had her baseball bat – which she'd like back by the way.'

They walked into town in silence.

'You must've felt awful, Melv. Not being able to say how you knew the truth about the Burkes,' Cas said eventually.

Melvin nodded. 'Things are beginning to connect, though. That's what Arnold reckoned was the key to avenging his murder. Making connections. We know now that our school is linked to Flogmore Hall.'

'Do you think Esther's a Burke?' asked Cas.

'I've always thought Esther was a berk,' replied Melvin.

They walked for a bit in silence.

Then Cas said, 'I couldn't sleep last night, I kept having nightmares. About Esther, deadheads . . .'

'I wish I had nightmares,' said Melvin.

'You *like* nightmares?' asked Cas, incredulously.

'They're better than dreams,' said Melvin.

'What do you mean?' asked Cas.

Melvin was about to tell her all about his dad. Then he remembered how quickly Cas could turn things into a joke. So he said nothing, but simply shrugged.

V

No one else has more right or reason to be in the school office, leafing through the members of 8GG's personal files. Nevertheless, he feels easier doing it after school, when the place is empty.

Perkins, Melvin. *Year 7 reports; Year 6 reports . . . He goes right back to the beginning of the file, to the form Mr and Mrs Perkins had filled in the day Melvin had entered the Reception Class at Smallham First School.*

You see, he hopes that there might be something, anything, to give him the clue he needs. He is convinced that somehow the boy shares the power which he and the others had believed was theirs and theirs alone.

Nothing.

He is about to return the file to the filing cabinet, when a handwritten note spills out onto the floor. He picks it up and reads it.

'Dear Miss Lowe . . .' *It's an old letter, dating from the boy's time at Smallham First School.* 'Melvin's dad left home last Friday and it looks as if he has gone for good. Melvin is obviously very upset. So if he is a bit weepy in class, I hope you will understand. Yours sincerely, Kate Perkins.' *It's the date that excites him, though. Twenty-fourth of March. The final piece of the plan has unexpectedly fallen into place.*

5

'No wonder the smiling boys had looked like deadheads, they *were* deadheads!'

'Fight! Fight!'

Melvin could hear the chant even before he had reached the school gates. He had a dreadful feeling he knew who was doing the fighting and what they were fighting about.

He turned into the playground. The whole school seemed to be there in one excited, pulsating throng. Melvin's feelings had been fifty per cent correct: yes, it was Cas and Kayleigh fighting, most definitely; but no, they weren't fighting about him. They were fighting about the baseball bat.

A whistle blew and the crowd parted grudgingly as Miss Smith (French and PE) waded into the mêlée. She picked Cas up with one hand and Kayleigh with the other. Then she shook them like a couple of bits of dripping washing. Melvin wondered if she was a descendant of Half-Hung Smith, whom Arnold had talked about.

'Mr Ranson's office,' she bawled.

And so into Esther's office they went.

When they came into the first lesson, Kayleigh shot Melvin a look that said, 'I'd like to kill you.' Cas shot him a look that said, 'And I'd like to bring you back to life, just for the pleasure of killing you

51

all over again.'

She cornered him in the cloakrooms at breaktime.

'It's all your fault, Perkins!'

'I didn't swap her baseball bat for my phone number!'

'No, you told her we'd been up Hogman's Thorn woods!'

'We had been up Hogman's Thorn woods!'

'Yes, but you didn't have to tell her that! Couldn't you have strung her along or something?'

Melvin felt out of his depth. Very much out of his depth.

'As it is,' Cas continued, her face like thunder, 'I've got a detention after school. You'll have to pick up my library book.'

'What library book?'

'It's for my History project,' Cas said. 'It's got to be picked up today or else they'll put it back in the store. And they close at four thirty today. Here's my ticket.'

'But I've got to go to Worthing – '

'Then you'll have to hurry.'

Melvin got plenty of funny looks during the day. Word had got round that Cas and Kayleigh had been fighting over him. Stacey Taylor even offered him the key to her dad's allotment shed: 'In case you need to hide from those two. That Cas is all mouth and big trouble. And Kayleigh's dad thumps any boy who so much as looks at her!'

At afternoon break, Pravi asked Melvin, 'How

do you get girls to fancy you?'

'How should I know?' Melvin replied. 'I'd like to know how to *stop* girls fancying you.'

After school Melvin walked into town with Pravi. It was a relief not to have to look out for Kayleigh. It was a relief, too, to know that he didn't have to worry about Esther. He would be busy for the next half hour supervising Kayleigh and Cas's detention.

'Where are you going?' asked Melvin, as they passed Pravi's parents' shop.

'Library,' replied Pravi. 'I'm going to check out your story about the Burkes.'

'You believe it, don't you, Pravi?'

Pravi shrugged. 'I hope you're right. It would certainly make my project a lot more interesting. Are you going to the library, too?'

Melvin couldn't deny it. They were already walking up the steps of the squat Victorian building.

Melvin handed Cas's reservation slip to the librarian.

The librarian looked over her glasses at Melvin with a deeply suspicious stare as she handed him Cas's book. 'Happy reading, Cassandra,' she said.

Melvin smiled sheepishly. Pravi guffawed. 'See you, Cassandra!' he called.

Melvin cursed under his breath. In truth, Cas's book wasn't so much a book as a box. Labelled *Miscellaneous Documents Relating to Smallham*

Voluntary Organisations & Societies 1850 – It was big; it was bulky. It weighed a ton.

Kayleigh and the real Cassandra Washbone stood on either side of Esther's office door, glowering at each other. The light above the door flashed DO NOT ENTER!!

Suddenly the door opened. Miss Smith (French and PE) came out. 'Ah yes,' she sniffed, 'you two.'

'Come in and wait in front of my desk,' called Esther severely. As if they would dare to wait anywhere else.

He went to the door and spoke in whispered tones to Miss Smith. Cas couldn't hear what he said but she heard Miss Smith's reply: 'No, no, that's quite all right, George.'

Cas pondered. Why does she call him George, when his name's Guy? Perhaps George is a false name. It bothered her.

'I want an essay from each of you entitled *Why It is Churlish to Fight About the Rightful Ownership of a Baseball Bat*,' said Esther. No one had ever called Esther an original thinker. 'Bring it to me in thirty minutes. I shall be in the staff room.'

Melvin sat down wearily on one of the little red flaps that served as a seat at the bus stop. There was no point in his visiting the *Smallham Gazette* offices, he knew. The murder he was investigating had been covered up; it wouldn't have been in the papers. But if he didn't go, he would be in trouble with the Gibbon. And now he had to lug Cas's stupid box of tricks all the way to Worthing and back. Not only that, it had started to rain – cold, heavy, wintry rain. Melvin shivered.

Just then there was a toot and the school minibus drew up. The driver leaned over and wound down the steamed-up passenger window.

'I thought that was you, Melvin.'

'Hello, Mr Gibbons.'

'You're waiting for the Worthing bus, I suppose?'

Melvin nodded, ruefully.

'Hop in. I'll whizz you over there.'

'Are you sure, sir?'

'Yes!' smiled the Gibbon. 'I haven't seen my old mate on the *Gazette* for ages; it'll be good to have a chat.'

Melvin climbed in.

The Gibbon didn't say anything. He seemed to Melvin to be anxious about something or other.

As they sped out of Smallham towards the by-pass, Melvin looked inside the *Miscellaneous Documents Relating to Smallham Voluntary Organisations & Societies 1850* – box. The first booklet in the box was entitled *Dib Dib Dob! A Silver Anniversary History of the 1st Smallham Wolf Club Pack 1935–1960*. Then there was a booklet about the Town Band – that was one for Cas's project, Melvin thought. He came next to a pamphlet called *The Smallham Coronation Souvenir 1953*. He flicked through it. A photograph in the centre spread suddenly made him start. The mock Tudor gables, the tall, narrow windows . . . and the caption confirmed it: *A Coronation Party was held at Hogman's Thorn House . . .*

In the foreground of the photograph was a tall, dark-haired woman in a shapeless dress. Melvin read some more of the caption: . . . *by kind permission of the owner . . .*

This was the granddaughter of Arnold's 'master' and murderer! The one he had called 'an evil old witch'! Melvin read on: . . . *Mrs Allbright.*

Melvin's head buzzed. Angie Allbright – who had so very nearly masterminded the deadheading of the New Age travellers. Her grandmother? It had to be! She was a descendant of Obadiah Burke, who had murdered Arnold!

'That's the connection!' muttered Melvin aloud.

'Sorry, did you say something, Melvin?' asked the Gibbon.

But Melvin didn't hear him. He was thinking; thinking back to the picture in Pravi's book. No wonder the smiling boys had looked like deadheads, they *were* deadheads! The evil power of the House had somehow been passed down through the generations from Obadiah Burke to Angie Allbright and no doubt Harry Summerskill, Darius O'Fee and –

Melvin's eye caught a further caption at the bottom of the page. *Mrs Allbright is pictured holding her infant grandson Guy.* Esther as a baby!

56

Melvin looked up and turned to the Gibbon. 'I've got some evidence, sir. And this is the source,' he grinned, triumphantly waving *The Smallham Coronation Souvenir 1953*.

There was a further caption at the bottom of the page: *Next to Mrs Allbright stands young Guy's mother and Mrs Allbright's daughter Mrs –*

Melvin just knew the word had to be *Ranson*, for the baby in Mrs Allbright's arms was Esther, surely? But the surname wasn't Ranson. It was – no, NO! Desperately, Melvin tried to convince himself that his eyes were playing tricks, but however much the letters of Obadiah Burke's great-great-grandson's surname danced before his eyes, they would not change.

Melvin broke into a cold sweat as he forced himself to raise his head and look up again.

It was only then that he realised something else wasn't quite right.

There was no traffic on the road.

There were no houses along the roadside.

'Sir . . . ?'

'Yes, Melvin?'

'This isn't the Worthing road!'

'You're quite right of course, Melvin. It isn't the Worthing road.'

'But you said you were taking me to Worthing!' protested Melvin, his voice breathless with terror.

The teacher fixed his steady gaze on his pupil. 'I lied to you, Melvin.'

57

The Smallham Coronation Souvenir 1953 slid from Melvin's shaking hands onto the floor of the minibus.

VI

Esther stands admiring the notice in the staff room at Sir Norman Burke Middle School. It is source of great joy to him that every member of his staff is attending the In-Service Training Course. It should guarantee a glowing testimonial for him in the OFSTED Inspector's report.

There is a timid knock at the door.

'Come!' calls Esther.

Cassandra Washbone and Kayleigh Foster shuffle into the staff room. Their heads are lowered and they each clutch a sheet of A4 paper in their right hands.

'Put them there,' instructs Esther, pointing to the grimy coffee table. 'I want no more of this nonsense, otherwise I shall be compelled to call in your respective parents. Is that understood?'

'Yes, Mr Ranson,' mumbles Kayleigh, contritely.

'Cassandra?' Esther coughs, a sure sign that he is about to put on what he considers as his strict, yet awe-inspiring voice.

But Cassandra doesn't reply. She hasn't even heard Esther's question, let alone had her awe inspired by the strict tone of his voice. She is staring open-mouthed at the large poster on the staff notice board, the very same poster Esther had been looking at with such satisfaction a few minutes earlier.

In-Serving Training Course: Hogman's Thorn House, *she reads.*

'Cassandra! Are you listening to me?' Esther puffs, crossly. 'Present yourself outside my office tomorrow morning at nine o'clock sharp!'

It all becomes suddenly and amazingly clear to Cas: the next group of intended deadheading victims is the staff of Sir Norman Burke Middle School and they are going to be willingly led to their fate by their own Head Teacher.

6

'She saw his eyes: they were as hard and as lifeless as buttons . . .'

Ellie opened the door. 'Mum!' she yelled. 'It's Melvin's girlfriend!'

Cas winced.

Mrs Perkins came through.

'Hello, Mrs Perkins, is Melvin in?'

Mrs Perkins frowned. 'I thought he was with you, Cassandra.'

Cas shook her head. 'He was going over to Worthing to the *Gazette* offices – '

'Yes, I know, he told me,' said Mrs Perkins anxiously. 'But it's gone eight now. You'd better come in. Hannah!' she called. 'Look after Ellie.'

Cas and Mrs Perkins sat in the kitchen. 'I expect he's got his head buried in some book, you know Melvin,' said Mrs Perkins, her attempts at a smile not totally able to conceal her fretfulness.

Cas knew Melvin. And she knew that he hadn't got his head stuck in a book. She knew that wherever he was, he was in dreadful danger.

'I'll ring the *Gazette*,' muttered Mrs Perkins, absent-mindedly. 'Now where's their number . . . Oh yes, the hamster.'

Perhaps worrying about Melvin has affected her mind, thought Cas, who for the life of her couldn't work out how Ellie's pet hamster was going to be able to tell them the number for the Worthing office of the *Gazette*.

Mrs Perkins opened the cage, scooped up a small brown furry bundle and dropped it into Cas's hands.

'His name's Liam,' said Mrs Perkins.

'Hi, Liam,' said Cas, stroking the bundle of fur gently. But Liam didn't even say 'Hello Cas,' let alone 'Oh and by the way, the number for the Worthing office of the *Gazette* is – '

'This is what I'm after,' muttered Mrs Perkins, pulling the sheet of newspaper from the bottom of Liam's cage, a sheet of newspaper that bore the title *Smallham Gazette*. She blew away a crusty covering of food, straw and hamster droppings. 'There!' she cried, stabbing her finger at a phone number.

She dialled. After a lot of uh-humming, yes-ing and no-ing, she put the receiver down. Cas knew what she was going to say. Even if she hadn't known it all along, she would've been able to tell it from Mrs Perkins' face.

'Melvin isn't at the *Gazette* offices,' she said quietly. 'In fact, he didn't keep his appointment. He never even went there.'

Which was why, instead of confronting Cas and Kayleigh in his office at nine o'clock sharp the next morning, Esther found himself facing the massed ranks of 8GG.

'By now you will have all heard the disturbing news about Melvin Perkins' disappearance,' he began. He indicated a tall, thin man in a shiny suit who stood on his left. 'This is Detective Inspector Jinks. He has a few questions to ask us all.'

Then he should begin with asking you just what you've done with him, you evil deadheader, thought Cas. She said nothing though. She sat looking down at her pencil case, afraid that if her eyes met Esther's, the hate and anger in them would alert him to the fact that she knew the dreadful truth.

'Now you were – I mean *are* – Melvin's friends,' began Detective Inspector Jinks, uncertainly. 'I want you to think, to think hard. Is there any reason Melvin should've disappeared? All we know is that Melvin didn't arrive for the appointment he had at the *Gazette* in Worthing. Was he unhappy – or upset about anything?'

'Yes!' called out a surprisingly loud and agitated voice. All eyes turned to Kayleigh Foster. 'The day before yesterday me and Melv had a row and I called him a pathetic little skunk and told him I wouldn't go out with him!' Twenty-eight gasps filled the electric atmosphere in 8GG's tutor group. Then Kayleigh burst into uncontrollable sobs and had to be helped to the girls' toilets by Jodie Jenkins.

Detective Inspector Jinks sighed. 'Has anybody else anything to offer?'

'I walked into town with him,' said Pravi. 'We

went to the library.'

'Can you remember the last thing you said to him,' asked Detective Inspector Jinks.

'Yes,' said Pravi, sadly.

'And what was that?'

'See you, Cassandra.'

The mid-morning news on South Downs TV led with 'Disappearance of Smallham Schoolboy'. A breathless reporter explained that the police believed 'Malcolm Pootkins aged thirteen had been jilted by his girlfriend.'

At about the same time, in Smallham Library, six vagrants, two school truants and an elderly lady who secretly took books off the shelves and wrote rude words in the margins all made a hurried exit as Detective Inspector Jinks and two uniformed police officers presented themselves at the issue desk.

'Do you recognise this boy?' asked Detective Inspector Jinks, thrusting a distinctly unflattering school photo of Melvin under the nose of the startled librarian. She was the kind of librarian who had a particular dislike of being startled.

'Yes,' replied the librarian starchily. 'He came in here late yesterday afternoon, trying to pass himself off as a girl.'

'You mean he was wearing a blouse and a skirt?'

The librarian looked over her glasses at Detective

Inspector Jinks as if he was some sort of pervert. 'No I do not!' she snapped. 'I mean he produced a girl's library ticket!'

'Are they different from boys' library tickets, then?' inquired Detective Inspector Jinks.

The librarian looked over her glasses at Detective Inspector Jinks as if he was not only some sort of pervert, but a particularly stupid sort of pervert. 'A particular girl's library ticket,' she replied, as patiently as she could.

'What particular girl?'

'Cassandra Washbone,' said the librarian.

The lunchtime news on South Downs TV led with 'New theory in Mystery Disappearance of Smallham Schoolboy'. The same reporter – now even more breathless – explained that the police now had evidence that 'Mervin Parkins aged fourteen had been seen in Smallham Library dressed in a blouse and a skirt.' The reporter was quick to add, however, that police were continuing to follow a number of leads.

'Why didn't you tell me you had asked Melvin to go to the library for you?' asked Detective Inspector Jinks, severely.

Cas shrugged sullenly.

'We want to find him as much as you do, Cassandra.'

Cas was trying to think – to think clearly. It wasn't

easy. She knew what could happen to Melvin once the deadheaders had hold of him – and they *did* have hold of him, she was sure of that. Out of the corner of her eye, she could see the poster announcing details of the In-Service Training Course. Not only that, but unless I can do something, she thought desperately, by the time the Easter holidays start, all the staff will be deadheads.

'Have you searched Hogman's Thorn House and the grounds?' she said at last.

'No, why?'

'Er . . .' She couldn't say *because that's probably where the deadheaders have taken him*; she couldn't say *because that's where he goes to meet his best friend – who, by the way, is the ghost of a Victorian juvenile delinquent.*

Instead she said: 'I know he goes up there on his bike a lot.'

Cas wandered out into the corridor, still deep in thought. So deep in thought, in fact, that she didn't see the caretaker's mop and bucket. Her shin caught the bucket's metal side and with a yelp of pain she crashed to the floor. She struggled to her feet, cursing and swearing under her breath.

The new temporary caretaker stood there holding his mop.

'Are you all right?' he asked.

Something in the tone of his query made Cas look up. She saw his eyes: they had a familiar look: they were as hard and as lifeless as buttons, just as his query had been. With a sickening lump rising in her throat, Cas realised that the temporary caretaker was a deadhead. The latest deadheading programme was under way. And this time they had Melvin.

Cas dived into the girls' toilets. She stood in front of the mirror, gripping the sides of the hand basin to steady her shaking self. She stared at herself for a few seconds, trying to grasp the magnitude of the events that were unfolding before her. Not only was Melvin in danger, every member of staff was! And once the staff were deadheads, how easy it would be for all their classes to become deadheads, too. And then it would only be a matter of time before the whole town was under the control of Esther and the rest of the deadheaders and their masters.

And despite her reputation as one of Sir Norman Burke Middle School's toughies, despite her judo brown belt, despite her size eight Cats, Cas was scared out of her mind. But perhaps there was one person, one member of staff who might be persuaded to think twice . . .

At lunchtime, she stayed in the classroom while the rest of 8GG rushed out.

'Mr Gibbons . . . ?'

The Gibbon looked up from his marking. 'Yes, Cassandra?'

'About Melvin. I think I know *why* he has disappeared.'

The Gibbon shuffled uncomfortably. 'Have you

told the police?' he asked.

'I can't.'

'Why not?'

'Because they wouldn't believe me, sir.'

The Gibbon frowned.

Cas took a deep breath and pitched straight in. 'It's all to do with Hogman's Thorn House, sir. I think Melvin's been kidnapped. Because of what he knows. About the people who run the House. Evil people. The same people who are organising your staff training course.'

The Gibbon narrowed his eyes. 'Go on . . .'

'You *will* believe me, sir, won't you? Even if it sounds as if I'm a complete dork.'

Almost unnoticed by Cas, the Gibbon closed the classroom door. 'Yes, I'll believe you, Cassandra. You don't mind if I tuck into my sandwiches, do you?'

Cas shook her head. 'It's like this, sir,' she began.

The Gibbon was unfastening his briefcase. Cas glanced across as he took out a neat square of silver foil. That was when she saw his name inked in, in large letters on the inside of his briefcase. Not just his surname though, but his first name: *Guy Gibbons*, she read.

With terrifying speed it dawned upon Cas that she had it all wrong. The reason Miss Smith called Esther George was that his first name was George. He wasn't Guy, the fourth deadheader, at all.

No, the fourth deadheader was her form tutor;

the man who lent his initials to their form's name – 8GG. The fourth deadheader was Mr Gibbons; Mr *Guy* Gibbons.

The fourth deadheader was sitting opposite her, saying, 'Go on, Cassandra, you were telling me about Hogman's Thorn House and some evil people up there.'

As they had promised five million people on local television news, the police were continuing to follow a number of other leads. One of these leads was tied around the neck of Cyril, an Alsatian sniffer dog who with five of his masters, together with their respective handlers, two teams of uniformed police officers, local volunteers, the latest piece of heat-seeking technology and a helicopter were searching the grounds of Hogman's Thorn House.

Plain-clothed officers wearing natty see-through gloves combed the House itself. Detective Inspector Jinks himself marvelled at the conference facilities therein and vowed to persuade his superiors to book Hogman's Thorn House for the next CID training course.

He was not overly bothered by the strange room containing surgical knives and scalpels, as the very helpful, but dull-eyed, security guard explained to him that a conference of eminent brain surgeons was due to be held the following week.

Of Melvin Perkins, he had found nothing. But all the while there flitted anxiously round him a scruffy boy who, if the Inspector had bothered to ask him, would have provided the information that Melvin Perkins had last been at Hogman's Thorn House four days ago. Detective Inspector Jinks didn't ask him, of course, for the simple reason that he couldn't see ghosts.

'Inspector!' It was a moment before the detective turned round. He had only just been promoted and still had to remember that when someone called 'Inspector!' they meant him.

'Mr Gibbons, how can I help?'

A chill March wind cut across the lawn and Detective Inspector Jinks pulled the collar of his coat closer about his neck.

'I think I might know of a motive for Melvin's disappearance.'

Detective Inspector Jinks raised one corner of an eyebrow, the way he'd been taught to while training to be a detective. 'Go on . . .'

'The thought only came to me this afternoon. I was thinking that the boy had seemed rather distracted of late. And then I remembered: it's the anniversary today of the day that Melvin's father left home. I know that Melvin still misses him. I think the lad's gone to find him.'

Dectective Inspector Jinks frowned. 'The mother mentioned nothing of this.'

'I rather imagine that she has tried to blot all memory of her husband's desertion from her mind.'

'Hmmm . . . Has anybody any idea where the boy

might have gone to try and find his father?'

'There was talk,' the Gibbon said airily, 'that his father was living in the States.'

Fifteen minutes later, every international airport in the country was put on alert and provided with details of Melvin Perkins Aged 13 Last Seen Wearing a Red Jumper and Carrying a Box Labelled *Miscellaneous Documents Relating to Smallham Voluntary Organisations & Societies 1850 –*

The early evening news on South Downs TV led with 'Absent Father Linked With Missing Boy Case'. The same reporter – now even more breathless – explained that police now had evidence that 'Merlin Pipkins aged nine had gone to the States to find his dad'. An expert explained just how easy it was to stow away on a jumbo jet. Another expert explained just how easy it was to get a forged passport.

On the same bulletin, Detective Inspector Jinks turned directly to the camera and appealed for anyone with news of Melvin's whereabouts to come forward; Mrs Perkins, her voice tearful and hesitant, asked Melvin to contact her, just to let her know he was all right and an ashen-faced Mr Guy Gibbons told everyone what a popular and likeable boy Melvin Perkins was.

Mrs Perkins and Hannah were sitting in the kitchen

when the doorbell went.

'I'll go, Mum,' said Hannah.

As she tugged at the front door, Hannah could feel her arms shaking. She was sure that whoever was there had news of her missing brother. The door gave way suddenly and Hannah started when she saw the young man on the doorstep. His hair was as flat as a doormat and a silver ring glinted in his left ear.

'Bunny!' gasped Hannah.

'Hi, Hannah. Er . . . Mum thought I should come over and tell you.'

'Tell me what?'

'The police are at our place.'

'Why?'

'Our Cas has disappeared.'

VII

*She tosses another log onto the already blazing fire
in a futile attempt to bring some warmth into the
farmhouse parlour.*

*'Angie, for goodness' sake, stop being so twitchy,'
snaps Guy.*

*She swears. 'We've just had PC Plod marching
through the house and grounds – not to mention a
hundred and one alsatians sniffing in every corner
and you tell me not to get twitchy?'*

*'They didn't find anything though, did they?' says
Guy.*

*'I think it'll turn out to be a blessing in disguise,'
agrees Harry. 'They've done their snooping. They
won't bother us now. We will be left in peace to
get on with the business in hand. The deadheading
business.'*

*Angie turns to Guy, 'You must deal with the boy
tonight,' she says. 'I mean deal with him for good!'*

*A slightest flicker of unease crosses Guy's eyes. It
is almost imperceptible, but Angie notices it.*

*'Angie's right.' Darius speaks for the first time.
'Get out to the barn and sort it out now, Guy.'*

He piles more straw about himself to keep in the

warmth. He's not had his hands or feet tied. But then, as he was told when he was first bundled into the place the night before, 'This part of the barn was built to house a couple of tons of prize bull, Melvin, so banish from your mind all thoughts of escape.'

Indeed, all four walls are half a metre thick. There is a small window high up just under the ceiling, but there is no way of reaching it. And the door, as Melvin has been told, was built to withstand the weight of a charging bull.

At first, more than anything else, Melvin had been angry. Angry that nothing made sense any more; angry that he didn't realise the Gibbon was the fourth deadheader; angrier still that his form tutor was someone he had liked and trusted.

He had been angry most of all though because he knew what his mum and sisters would be going through, discovering that he had gone. They would feel as he had, the day his dad had left home. He had hated the thought of them going through that again.

Now, after twenty-four hours in the barn, the anger is giving way to fear.

The Gibbon and his cronies are all deadheaders, after all. He has not been brought out here to this isolated farm for a country holiday.

He knows what they are capable of. They have inherited a lust for power and evil that was first manifested in their common ancestor, Obadiah Burke. And Obadiah Burke was capable of murder.

74

Melvin's thoughts are interrupted by the sound of the heavy oak door being eased open on its creaking hinges.

The Gibbon flashes a torch into his eyes.

'Melvin,' he says. 'Your time has come.'

There is a terrible finality about his words.

7

'Let's get on with it and put him out of his misery...'

Melvin tried to make out the direction they were going in, but it was difficult. The Gibbon had sat him on the floor in the back of the minibus and tied him to the base of one of the seats. Occasionally he caught a brief glimpse of the moon through one of the windows, but no sooner had it appeared than another thick bank of cloud would come scudding across it again. The gag the Gibbon had put round his mouth made him feel sick. He was weary. He wanted it all to be over. The ride. The deadheading. Whatever they were going to do to him.

Eventually the minibus slowed down and the Gibbon turned sharply off the road. Melvin heard the outside of the bus being scraped and scratched. They were in some sort of wood, he guessed.

The Gibbon stopped the minibus, opened up the back and untied Melvin's legs from the seat.

'Walk,' ordered the Gibbon. 'And it's no good trying to run anywhere. Your hands are tied, so you'll lose your balance and fall over. Mind you, you should know that, if you remember your Key Stage Three Science.'

There would have been little point in Melvin trying to run for it anyway; the wood they were parked in was so dark and thick, he would have soon stumbled and fallen.

As they pushed on, the shadowy outlines of the trees began to take a peculiar sense of familiarity. The Gibbon must have sensed this, for he said: 'Do you know the way from here?'

Of course he did. There directly in front of them was the oak tree up which he had climbed to get into the grounds of Hogman's Thorn House. They were in Hogman's Thorn.

They reached the oak tree. The Gibbon tied the rope with which he had bound Melvin to the minibus seat round his right ankle, leaving a free end to grip in his own hand. Then he untied Melvin's hands.

'Up you go,' he commanded. 'And if you so much as try anything, I'll pull the rope.'

Melvin climbed the tree. The Gibbon followed. Out along the branch that overhung the garden they went. Melvin was astonished to see another rope already in place; securely knotted to the branch.

'Down you go – I shall be right behind you,' threatened the Gibbon.

They both dropped to the ground. What are we doing this for? thought Melvin. Why doesn't he take me through the front door?

The Gibbon untied Melvin's gag. Melvin tried to open his mouth, but his jaw and lips were sore.

'Shouting won't help,' said the Gibbon, 'you'd be better saving your breath for the next climb.

Come on!'

Through the bushes they went, until they reached the back wall of the house – the wall that faced the woods.

'Up!' The Gibbon spoke sharply, but his voice was quieter now. He was pointing to the iron fire escape.

Melvin obeyed. Step after cautious step he took, gripping each rung firmly. All the time he was expecting the rope that was tied round his ankle to be yanked hard and to find himself plummeting helplessly towards the ground.

The nearer the roof they got, the colder Melvin's fingers became. The chill wind stung his ears.

'Any false move now and you'll be over the edge,' muttered the Gibbon as they crawled off the ladder onto the roof. He tapped gently with his knuckles on a skylight, which then began to rise slowly. Someone was pushing it open from inside. The Gibbon lifted up the skylight until it swung right back on the roof. 'Jump in,' he told Melvin. 'There's a mattress to land on. Roll over quickly unless you want me landing on top of you.'

There was no choice. Melvin jumped.

He landed with a jolt, as promised, on some kind of mattress. He rolled over just as the Gibbon thudded down beside him.

'Melv?' called out a voice behind him.

There was only one person who called him 'Melv' like that, Melvin knew. He struggled to speak, to

78

say 'Cas?' but when he opened his mouth, only a gurgle came out.

'Are you okay, Melvin?' Another voice. Another oh-so-familiar voice.

'Hannah!' Melvin tried to say, but still he could only gurgle.

Cas shone a small pocket torch into his face. 'What's wrong with his voice?'

'Stiff jaw I expect, from the gag,' said the Gibbon.

'You gagged him?'

'Of course I did!' There was a tinge of emotion in the Gibbon's voice, that could almost have been embarrassment or even guilt. 'We can't take any risks!'

Melvin could hear somebody else working with the stick to get the skylight shut. 'Careful, don't let it bang, Bunny,' the Gibbon warned, 'it's ancient.'

'Let's get on with it and put him out of his misery,' Cas said.

'It could take some time,' said Bunny uneasily.

'Don't try to say anything, Melv,' said Cas. 'We'll do the talking.'

Melvin leant back against the pitched roof of the attic and closed his eyes. It was as much as he could do to concentrate on what Cas was saying.

She explained how she had stumbled onto the fact that the Sir Norman Burke Middle School Staff training course was being held at Hogman's Thorn House . . .

'. . . And then Mr Gibbons got out his sandwiches.' She shivered. 'And I found out that he, not Esther, was the fourth deadheader.'

'That must've been a terrible moment, Cas,' sighed Bunny.

'You're telling me,' agreed Cas. 'They were Liver Sausage and Pickled Onion. And then . . . are you listening, Melv?'

Cas shone her torch in Melvin's face. He sat bolt upright. His head was swimming. Only a few minutes ago, this evil man – this deadheader – who had imprisoned him, bound and gagged him, was threatening to push him off the roof. Now Cas, Hannah and Bunny were treating him like an old friend – and they knew he was the fourth dead-header. Had the Gibbon deadheaded them? He must have done! And now they were all softening him – Melvin – up for the same treatment.

'Yes, Melvin,' said the Gibbon. 'I am the fourth deadheader – at least I would be if I chose to be. The other three, Angie, Darius and Harry, are my cousins. We have in common a great-great-grand-father – Obadiah Burke. The power that he first divined in Hogman's Thorn and harnessed for his own use has been passed down to us.'

Now that his eyes had grown accustomed to the dark, Melvin could make out the ghostly shapes of Cas, Bunny, Hannah and the Gibbon. He could also see that Hannah and Bunny were holding hands. All four were looking intently at him. They're trying to hypnotise me, Melvin thought to himself, but they won't; they can't, not in the dark.

'But Mr Gibbons isn't a deadheader, he's on our side,' Cas said.

Melvin could have wept when he heard her say this.

'I didn't believe him at first,' Cas went on, 'but then I realised he was telling the truth. I could tell it from his eyes. They're not cold and piercing, not like his cousins' eyes.'

Melvin hid his face in his hands. Not only was Cas a deadhead, her brain had completely gone.

The Gibbon spoke. 'I knew that Cassandra's brother, your sister and Pravi Patel had fought the deadheads before, so I agreed to meet them all after school.'

Melvin looked around. There was no sign of Pravi.

'But we had a problem with Pravi,' said the Gibbon, darkly.

Yes, thought Melvin, I bet you couldn't deadhead *him*.

'I went round to his place after school,' said Cas. 'He was just going down the rec.' She paused. 'With Kayleigh Foster. There was no way we could let Kayleigh in on something as dangerous as this.'

Melvin didn't believe her. Pravi – with Kayleigh Foster? Did Cas really expect him to believe that? It only went to show what a complete deadhead she had become.

Bunny took up the story. 'It seemed obvious that

if the deadheaders were to be defeated, you had to be involved and you had to be here – at the House. This is where their power – and your power – lies.'

'But Mr Gibbons reckoned you didn't trust him any more,' explained Hannah.

Too right I don't, thought Melvin, bitterly.

'So we agreed to be here, despite the obvious danger we are in,' Cas said grandly, 'because we knew that once we'd explained everything to you, you'd understand.'

'You idiots!' said Melvin. 'Don't you see? He's duped you. All of you! He kidnapped me! Locked me up in a filthy old barn!'

'I'm sorry, Melvin, I had to do it that way,' the Gibbon said, quietly. 'If I hadn't pretended to have kidnapped you, Darius or Angie or Harry would have done it – for real. And if that had happened, you wouldn't be sitting here now... The dead-heading programme is reaching its final and most important phase. Anything that stands in their way is to be eliminated. That's why we came here the way we did. There are security cameras on the front door. If we'd turned up there, our arrival would've been recorded for Angie and Darius' benefit on video. It's as simple as that.'

'Perhaps it would be a good idea if you told Melvin about the Black Book,' suggested Cas.

'Yes, you're right,' the Gibbon nodded. He took a deep breath. 'A few years ago my grandmother, the one you saw in that picture in *The Coronation*

82

Year Book, Melvin, gathered the four of us together. "I don't have long for this world," she told us, "so it's time you were told about the Black Book." The Black Book, she explained, was started by Obadiah Burke and continued by his son Norman. In this Black Book were set out various notes on their discoveries about Hogman's Thorn and its strange powers.'

'We're on a ley line, Melv!' interrupted Cas, excitedly.

'Cas,' said Bunny, 'don't you know it's rude to butt in when your teacher's talking?'

Cas stuck out her tongue at her brother.

'Cas is right,' the Gibbon went on. 'Obadiah discovered that Hogman's Thorn is on a ley line. These are straight lines that run across the country. You often find churches on them.'

'And UFOs are often seen near them,' said Bunny.

'Now who's interrupting,' growled Cas.

'What is certain,' said the Gibbon, sounding more and more like a teacher as he went on, 'is that underneath our ley line is a ridge of chalk, dotted with various springs.'

'Boing!' said Cas. Now that the Gibbon was speaking like a teacher, Cas had suddenly reverted to being a P.W.S.T. Everyone ignored her – including the Gibbon.

'Our ancient ancestors settled near these springs – for the obvious reason that they provided them with water. They set up their pagan places of worship and later, their churches. Hogman's Thorn is one of these ancient places. And whether it gets its power from the ley line itself or from the collective spirit of our ancestors, I don't know. Obadiah didn't either. He developed a kind of mesmerism which he used to brainwash the boys in the school.'

'Just like Harry Summerskill and his subliminal imaging,' said Bunny.

'In the Black Book,' the Gibbon continued, 'Obadiah describes how the mesmerism only worked when practised along a line running north to south within the House. He also discovered that it was especially powerful when practised by members of the family together. That's why Obadiah and Norman worked so closely together. And why they always worked here. We were all very excited, of course. If the kind of primitive energy that Hogman's Thorn could give us was applied to modern technologies, then untold power and wealth would be ours. Of course, the way they described it at first sounded fine. People would be deadheaded, but it would be for their own good. They would become better, brainier people – '

'Remember the Genius Academy?' whispered Hannah.

'But the more Angie and Darius and Harry talked about it, the more evil it became. And in turn they became more ruthless, more power crazy. They talked of selling their power and skill to the highest bidder.' The Gibbon seem to shiver. 'And that's when I started to become uneasy,' he said. 'I had to stop them, I knew. But how? They were going to create deadheads at any cost. I was expendable. I had to pretend to go along with their schemes and hope some way would present itself of halting the deadheading programme – and the Burke inheritance – for ever.'

Suddenly, Melvin jumped and Cas's hand immediately went to the zip of her jacket. She pulled out Kayleigh's baseball bat.

'Don't be stupid, I'm not going to try to take you all on single-handed,' muttered Melvin.

What had caused him to start was the appearance of a fifth person, who to Melvin's eyes was much more distinct than any of the other shadowy figures in the room. But then, ghosts are often at their most apparent in the dark.

'Mind if I join you, old fellow?' said Arnold. 'You would appear to be in a spot of bother.'

Arnold sat down.

The Gibbon looked around as if he could sense something in the atmosphere. Then he abruptly turned to Melvin. 'And now,' he said, steadily, without once averting his gaze, 'I think there is a way of stopping the deadheading programme. I probably don't need to tell you this, Melvin, but that way is through you.'

Melvin sighed. The thought flashed through his mind, that less than a year ago, he was able quite happily to live out Perkins' First Law of Survival (Keep Your Head Down) with no bother at all. Now here he was sitting with a deadheader, a Victorian ghost, the class Person-What-Spells-Trouble, her freaky brother and most incredible of all, his big sister, Horrible Hannah – being told that it was his job to save the world.

'Everything Mr Gibbons has said is true,' said Hannah, eventually.

'Don't listen to her, Perkins!' implored Arnold. 'Don't trust him! Don't trust any of them!'

'I don't trust you. Any of you!' Melvin shouted.

'Look, Melv, you great dollop,' reasoned Cas, 'if we don't stop the deadheads this time, they're going to deadhead all the staff at school. Then getting the kids will be a cinch. And after that the parents. But to do anything we need you.'

Melvin ignored her. He turned and looked the Gibbon right in the eyes. 'I trusted you once, Mr Gibbons. I am not going to trust you again.' Melvin felt weary and defeated, but curiously, despite himself he found his voice becoming more assured, more determined. 'I can't fight all four of you. But remember this, Mr Gibbons. Your cousins have tried to deadhead me before. And they have failed. There may be four of you, but I am not alone.'

'He means he's got Arnold to help him,' muttered Cas.

'Who's Arnold?' asked the Gibbon, sharply.

'Tell him, Melv,' said Cas.

Melvin shot Cas a look of fury.

'No.'

'Tell him, Perkins,' Melvin heard Arnold say. 'Tell him his filthy blood relative murdered an innocent orphan.'

'Arnold is a ghost,' said Melvin quietly, but firmly. He turned with a hateful glance to the Gibbon. 'He was murdered by Obadiah Burke – your great-great-grandfather.'

'And is he in this room now?' asked the Gibbon. Melvin nodded.

'Scruffy? Orange mophead? Trousers ripped right up to the knee, collarless shirt?' enquired the Gibbon.

'Punch the villain on the nose!' roared Arnold.

'Yes,' stammered Melvin, in answer to the Gibbon. His mind was a whirl. 'How do you know what he looks like? Can you see him?'

'I met him myself, once,' said the Gibbon. 'When I was a bit younger than you, Melvin. We were visiting Gran. We didn't come very often; my father thought my gran was an evil old witch – and he was right. Anyway, I was in the shrubbery when I saw this pale figure. I knew he was a ghost.'

'Did you talk to him?' asked an excited Cas.

'No,' replied the Gibbon. 'I think he tried to say something to me, but I couldn't hear what it was.'

'Yes, I remember,' Melvin heard Arnold whisper. 'A small boy. I thought he might be the one to help. The one to avenge my death. I could tell by his aura that he came from the light side of the House; not the dark, the evil side, you understand. But he could only see me, he couldn't hear me.' Then so quietly, it almost seemed as if it came not from Arnold, but from somewhere deep inside himself, Melvin heard his ghost-friend say, 'I was wrong. You can trust him, Perkins, old chap. You *must* trust him.'

There was a long silence while everyone waited for Melvin to say something. When he finally spoke, it was directly to his sister. 'What's happened to Mum and Ellie?'

'Ellie and Mum are at Gran's,' said Hannah. 'Ellie's okay. And so is Mum – now.'

'Now?'

'Your mum was frantic,' said Bunny, rather uneasily, 'so Hannah rang her and said that you'd rung my flat.'

'Why would I do that?'

'Because . . . er . . . we said you and Cas had run off together.'

'What!' Melvin felt himself turning beetroot.

'I tried to brain him, honestly,' shrugged Cas.

'We told your mum that you had seen the error of your ways, that you were staying with our Aunt Esme and would be back home sometime tomorrow.'

'And not to tell the police,' added Hannah.

'Then I told our mum the same story,' said Bunny. 'Except, of course, I told her you and Cas were staying with *your* Aunt Esme.'

'But I haven't got an Aunt Esme,' protested Melvin.

'Neither have we,' replied Cas. 'She's imaginary, to stop our mums from worrying. She sounds a very kind and sensible sort of old biddy, Aunt Esme, don't you think?'

'But how are we going to stop the deadheaders?' asked Melvin.

'I don't know,' said the Gibbon, anxiously. 'But the Sir Norman Burke staff arrive for the so-called In-Service Training Course straight after lunch. We must have a plan in place by then. Bunny, Hannah, you must get to see me at the school tomorrow lunchtime. You can tell me then what ideas you have come up with. I shall be coming up here mid-afternoon, supposedly preparing for the training course. Darius, Angie and Harry won't be along till later. They'll have the "broker" in tow.'

'Broker?' asked Melvin.

'This time, there will be a broker with them, someone who will take deadheading – the Burke inheritance – into the wider world.'

'The whole world's going to be deadheaded?' asked Melvin.

'Probably not,' said the Gibbon. 'But the Smallham deadheading experiment is only the beginning. Once this broker has seen deadheading work, Darius, Harry and Angie will be able to sell their powers to the highest bidder, whether that's a corrupt government or a criminal organisation or even a multi-national company. Anyway, while Darius and Angie entertain him, Harry will carry out stage one of the deadheading process.'

'Won't Esther and the rest of the staff recognise him?' asked Melvin. 'They all saw him during the WhoppaShoppa business.'

'They won't recognise his face at all,' said the Gibbon. 'He'll be wearing one of the deadheading masks. Now, you'll be safe enough here until people start arriving tomorrow. Just stay away from the cameras on the front of the house. If Angie, Darius, Harry or any of their deadheads catch any of you, then that will be it. Melvin, let me have your school tie, please.'

'Why?'

'It might help me sound convincing when I tell them that you are no longer ...'

'No longer what?'

'Just ... no longer,' said the Gibbon, gravely. 'Now, I've already stayed far too long. They will be waiting for me back at the farm. The last thing we want is for Angie and the others to get suspicious about me.'

With that chilling thought, the Gibbon stood lightly on Bunny's back, hoisted himself up and in a couple of seconds was out onto the roof and letting the skylight down behind him.

VIII

The school minibus roars off out of the farmyard in the spring morning sunshine. Angie goes back inside to the kitchen and shuts the door behind her. Her dark eyes brood intently. Harry notices her unease.

'Angie?' he inquires. Of late it has been Angie who has been their guiding force, who has driven them on, provided them with the self-belief they need to see this wonderful venture through to its natural conclusion. Surely she is not having doubts; not now?

Angie ignores Harry. Only when Darius comes through to the kitchen does she usher them both to sit down.

'I do not trust Guy,' is all she says.

Darius and Harry try to measure the weight of what she is saying. Guy is their cousin; Guy is one of them; Guy is an inheritor; Guy is party to the secrets of the Black Book.

'Where was he last night?' asks Angie.

'He told us. Disposing of the boy. Over in the old chalk pits,' says Harry hesitantly.

'Yes. That's what he told us. But last night was wet, remember? If Guy had been to the chalk pits the wheel arches on that minibus would have been white. So would his shoes and the mats in the cab. But

under the wheel arches and on the floor of the cab is not chalk, but mud; leaves, twigs. Wherever Guy was last night, it wasn't the old chalk pits.'

'I can't see him backing out now, not now that success is within our sights,' reasons Darius.

'I don't think for one moment he is backing out,' replies Angie. Such is the singlemindedness of her own belief in the deadheading programme – and more importantly in the power and wealth it will bring – that she cannot fathom how anyone else could think differently. 'No, I believe Guy thinks that he can cut us out.'

'How?' asks Darius increduously.

'It must be something to do with the boy. That is why he hasn't disposed of him. There can be no other rational explanation.'

'But for the boy to have power, he must be a descendant of Obadiah. We've checked the Black Book. Every descendant has been traced. He does not figure!'

Angie sighs. 'He has some kind of power, and it's linked to the House, that is for certain. And Guy is lying to us; that is for certain. The victims arrive this afternoon, as does our broker.'

'Then a watch must be put on Guy,' says Darius.

'Yes,' agrees Harry.

'I have already arranged it,' says Angie, steadily. 'Our "school caretaker" has been instructed. Guy will not be able to make a single move today, without it being reported to one of us.' She takes a small bag

from the Welsh dresser. 'If my suspicions are right, as I fear they are, then the ultimate step will have to be taken.' She hands Darius the bag. He peers inside, then looks up at Angie in horror.

'No, no! I can't! An anonymous face is hard enough, but not this one!'

'You can, and you will. Our goal is within our grasp. Nothing must be allowed to stop us now.' There is not the slightest trace of self-doubt in her voice. 'Nothing will stop us now.'

8

'And then ... came the slow, regular pad-pad of heavy boots on polished wood.'

Melvin lay on his back and looked up through the skylight towards the morning sun. A seagull, tempted inland by the strong wind, sat in the middle of the plastic trying to peck its way in.

Arnold was nowhere to be seen. Hannah lay curled up asleep in a tatty blanket. Bunny sat crossed-legged and perfectly still, his eyes closed.

'He's practising Zho'neng-Do,' explained Cas, as she joined Melvin. Melvin knew all about Zho'neng-Do; nine months ago, it had been his mum's latest fad.

'He's trying to get in touch with his inner self,' Cas went on, 'though why he can't send a fax like anyone else, I don't know.'

'Shut your face, our kid,' growled Bunny, good-naturedly.

'Ah, he's found his inner self,' said Cas. She paused. 'What are we going to do, Melv?'

'I've been thinking,' said Melvin.

'So that's why there's steam coming out of your ears!'

'Shut your face, our kid,' growled Bunny again, still good-naturedly, still with his eyes shut. 'What have you been thinking about, Melvin?'

'How I can avenge Arnold's death.'

'Don't you think you should be thinking about how to stop the deadheaders?' snapped Cas. 'Okay, it's a shame about Arnold having been murdered and all that, but he is dead! We're very much alive and I want to stay that way!'

Suddenly, Arnold flitted in. 'Perkins!' he yelled, agitatedly. 'There are two ugly fellows searching the building!'

'Sssssh,' said Melvin.

'Sssssh yourself!'

'Sssssh!' The strength and tone of Melvin's voice gave Cas no choice but to shut up. 'The guards are on their way!'

'I can't hear any – ooargh!' Cas broke off in mid-sentence as Bunny leapt to his feet and put his hands round her throat.

They held their breath and listened – and could hear nothing but the uncomfortable silence that seems to surround you when you are in a place of danger.

And then, quietly at first, came the slow, regular pad-pad of heavy boots on polished wood. Everyone sat rigid as dolls, as less than a metre below them, the deadhead guards stomped along. A sliver of torchlight burst through the ventilation grille in the attic floor. Hannah let out a gasp. But the thudding footsteps became quieter, until eventually they couldn't be heard at all.

'They've gone,' said Arnold.

'It's okay,' said Melvin.

'Thanks for the warning, Melvin,' said Bunny.

'Thanks for the warning, Arnold,' said Cas, meekly.

'From now on,' said Bunny, 'we talk in whispers. We'll be safe enough, so long as we're quiet. So, we do not move about unnecessarily.' There was a tremor in his voice. 'Go on, Melvin . . .'

Melvin took a deep breath. 'Arnold is the original link with Obadiah Burke. Perhaps some of his evil is still lingering on through Arnold. As if it's through him that the power of the ley line or whatever transmits itself into Darius, Angie and Harry. Perhaps the deadheaders will only be stopped when I finally manage to avenge Arnold's murder.'

'Right, so when someone wants revenge, like Arnold does, what are they after?' asked Bunny.

'I suppose what he really wants is for Obadiah Burke to be punished. But Obadiah Burke is dead,' Cas pointed out.

'There is a dark side to the power of Hogman's Thorn House, a power that Obadiah discovered and that lives on through Arnold and is being tapped by Darius, Angie and Harry. There is also a light side to the power – '

'Which lives on through you, Melvin,' said Bunny.

'But the deadheading experiments, the subliminal imaging, the virtual reality machine, the masks, all harness the dark power and they all had to be done in *darkened* rooms.' Melvin didn't know from where

96

deep inside him the idea was coming from; he just knew it felt right. 'Supposing we could light the dark side of the power.'

'Eh?' Cas was lost.

'Light will reveal,' murmured Bunny.

'Oh no, he's back to his Zho'neng-Do,' sighed Cas.

'No, he's right!' said Melvin, excitedly. 'If everybody knew the truth about the Flogmore Hall and how Arnold had been murdered, then he would feel that some justice had been done. And perhaps that would free his spirit.'

'And once his spirit had been freed, he wouldn't be around here any more, acting as a channel for the powers of Obadiah Burke?' suggested Cas.

'Something like that,' mumbled Melvin, suddenly unsure of himself. Suddenly aware, for the first time, that if he was right, he would soon lose his Victorian friend.

'Yes, Perkins!' Melvin heard Arnold whispering excitedly. 'Tell the world the truth about my murderers. You are right! *The truth shall make you free*, that is what is written in the Scriptures.'

'Even if you're right, who will believe us?' asked Cas, glumly. 'We haven't got any evidence that the Burkes murdered Arnold. What are you going to tell them? "My friend Arnold the ghost says it's true"?'

Nobody said anything. Hannah snored quietly. Bunny returned to his meditating. Cas stared at the ceiling, as if she were trying to find inspiration in the rafters. Melvin cocked his ear to one side as if he were listening to somebody talking to him. He was. He was listening to Arnold.

'Perkins, believe me, it all happened. They would take us to the Ice House to flog us. Some were locked up for days in there. That's where they carried out the thrashing that killed me.'

'My friend Arnold the ghost says he was murdered in the Ice House,' Melvin said.

'What's the Ice House?' asked Cas.

'Dunno, he hasn't told me yet,' replied Melvin.

'It's a Victorian idea – an underground room, built to keep food cool in,' said Bunny.

'And it's in the far corner of the garden, on the dark side of the house,' Melvin heard Arnold saying.

'If this evidence is what we need, then there is only one thing for it,' said Cas. 'We must check out this Ice House. There might be something there.'

Bunny nodded in agreement.

'No, Perkins,' Arnold whispered, with sheer panic in his voice, 'I cannot let you go there. It is a terrible place. A terrible place!'

But Melvin quietly got to his feet. Cas stood up, too.

'I'm coming with you, Melv,' she said.

'No!' said Arnold.

'No,' said Bunny.

'I'm going with him,' said Cas.

'What for?' asked Melvin.

'I've got Kayleigh's baseball bat tucked in my jacket. I've also got a brown belt in judo. You might be in need of some protection, Melv.'

Bunny sighed. He knew when he was a beaten man, which, when it came to his sister getting her own way, was just about every time. 'Given that Ice Houses by their very nature tend to be windowless, you may well need this, too,' he said, handing Melvin a torch.

It was while Melvin was on Bunny's shoulders, just about to hoist himself onto the roof to join Cas, that Hannah woke up. She saw her little brother inching his way out of the skylight and panicked. She opened her mouth and screamed. Bunny dived over to her and clasped a firm hand over her mouth.

The uneasy silence that followed only served to prove just how loud and piercing Hannah's cry had been.

IX

They stand either side of the main doors in Hogman's Thorn House. They look hard at each other. Then they look up. They nod surely at each other and make their slow and steady way up the staircase.

Quietly, steadily they open then close the doors to each upstairs room. They stand together on the top floor corridor.

Only now do they look up to the ceiling and see the trap door to the attic.

A grim smile crosses each of their faces.

One of them goes back downstairs. He knows where the stepladder is kept.

9

'The watchmen,' shouted Arnold. 'They're by the ladder!'

Melvin followed Arnold; Cas followed Melvin along the back of the house, the dark side of the house that saw no sun. On along the back of the outbuildings, the flagstones under their feet were damp and mossy; the air, as it always was hereabouts, chill.

'Perkins, if you insist on going into the Ice House, I must count you either as a fool or a friend.'

'Count me as both,' said Melvin.

Right at the far end of the garden, in a dark corner watched over by the trees on the far side of the wall, the ground swelled up into a large mound. The mound itself was a mass of matted, rank bracken and brambles. In the front of the mound was a rotting wooden door.

'It's open!' declared Cas.

'The police must've looked inside it when they were searching for me,' said Melvin.

'Careful, there are steps down,' warned Arnold. He stood back from the entrance. 'No, no, I'll not come in with you.'

Melvin shivered. It was a disturbing thing to see a ghost, who after all could feel no pain, troubled to the point of terror.

Inside the Ice House, it was dark and cold, but

surprisingly dry. The brick structure had held good for over a hundred years.

'Melv?' Cas sounded as though her teeth were chattering. 'Hannah's scream – those guards wouldn't have heard it, would they?'

'No, no . . .' said Melvin, trying to sound more confident than he felt. 'Bunny shut her up pretty quickly. And they were probably three floors away, at the front of the house.'

'Yes, I suppose so,' agreed Cas, unable to hide the doubt in her voice.

Melvin flashed the torch around. Empty walls were all he could see. They were pitted with gashes and small holes.

'Nothing,' he murmured. 'Nothing.'

'Shine the torch down there again,' said Cas suddenly. 'In the corner.'

In the thin beam, Melvin saw what Cas had glimpsed. The holes and gashes were not natural, but made by human hand. They were the shapes of letter and numbers.

'Graffiti,' whispered Cas.

The torch caught a large group of letters in its beam.

'D H. BEAT WITH STICKS. JAN 80,' read Melvin, aloud.

Cas grabbed the torch from Melvin and flashed it along the wall: E.K. WIPPT. FEB 80. 10 TMES. P M FLOGGED. HIS BLUD ON FLOR.

And so it went on, a grisly history of Flogmore

102

Hall School: a gruesome testimony against its cruel master, Obadiah Burke, had been etched into the walls of the Ice House, by as many of his victims as could write.

'Look!' cried Cas.

She was pointing to a carving low down on the wall, right by the corner.

Melvin traced the letters with his finger: 'OUR FREN, A T. KILLED BY MSTRS HAND,' he whispered. 'A T – Arnold Thomas.'

'Why didn't he tell you about this?' asked Cas.

'He's not been in here since the day over a hundred years ago when he received his last flogging,' said Melvin. 'And even if he had, none of this would have meant anything to him. Arnold's pretty hot when it comes to quoting the Bible, but he can't read.'

'It's a horrible place,' whispered Cas, suddenly. 'I could feel it as soon as we came in. Let's get back to the others.'

Outside the air was not any noticeably warmer than it had been in the Ice House. They had just passed the rear of the outbuildings when Arnold ushered Melvin back behind a conifer hedge. Melvin grabbed a startled Cas by the hand and hauled her down behind the hedge with him.

'The watchmen,' shouted Arnold. 'They're by the ladder!'

Through the hedge Melvin could make out two large men in uniform peering up at the fire escape.

Melvin was surprised to find himself still gripping Cas firmly by the hand. It was more than ten minutes before Arnold signalled the all-clear. Melvin pulled Cas towards the wall, all the time keeping hidden amongst the bushes, all the time following the inside of the wall around to the front gates. There they sat down and waited. Arnold appeared and stood quite still in front of them.

'The wind is getting up, Perkins,' he said. 'And that is always a sign that changes are afoot. You notice how quiet it is? Not one bird singing.'

Melvin listened. Arnold was right.

'Not one bird singing,' he repeated to Cas.

'What are you on about now, Melv?'

'That's what Arnold says.'

'Tell him he'd be more usefully employed keeping tabs on the guards.'

'For goodness' sake, go and keep tabs on the guards,' snapped Melvin.

Arnold muttered something that Melvin took to be a Victorian swear word and flitted off.

The wind grew stronger, the sky darker, the air more chill. They sat for what seemed like a lifetime amongst the twigs and rotting leaves that made up the rough ground of the shrubbery just inside the gates.

'Do you remember what the Gibbon said?' began Cas, eventually.

'Of course I do,' said Melvin. ' "If they catch any of you, that'll be it." '

'Melv . . . ?'

Melvin knew exactly what was going through Cas's mind: it was going through his, too. 'Oh, Hannah can handle herself,' he said, airily. 'Look . . .' He pulled up his sleeve and showed Cas his arm. 'See that scar?'

'What scar?'

'There!' Melvin pointed to a faint slightly curved indenture on the fleshy bit of his forearm. 'That's where Hannah left her mark. When I was about six. We were having a fight and she bit me. I shall carry that mark with me for the rest of my life.'

'If you intend to show it to people,' said Cas, 'you'd better carry a magnifying glass with you.'

'Ha,' grunted Melvin. 'Well, let me tell you, Washbone, that scar is important to me, because it's individual, that's what it is. I look at it and know that I'm *me*.'

'And just who are you, Melvin Perkins?' asked Cas cryptically.

'Eh?'

'You have these powers. Not only that, you can see Arnold. Why?'

Melvin shrugged.

'You know the obvious answer, of course.'

Melvin nodded. 'But I'm not related to the Burkes, I'm sure of it. Hannah did our family tree once. There were no Burkes on it. None.'

Cas sighed. 'Perhaps that why I like you, Melv.'

'Eh?'

105

'Neither of us knows who we really are.'

'What do you mean?' Melvin frowned. 'You know who you are, Cassandra Washbone, daughter of Councillor Mrs Washbone and Mr Washbone. Brother of Bunny – sorry, Warren – '

'No,' said Cas. 'I'm not. I'm adopted.'

Melvin looked Cas full in the face. 'You don't know who your real mum is?'

Cas shook her head. 'No, I'm not allowed, by law. Not until I'm eighteen.'

'Do you think she'll be like you?' asked Melvin.

'I don't know. Are you like your mum and dad?'

'I'm like my mum in some ways, I suppose,' said Melvin. 'Though she is a bit scatty. And my dad . . .' He tried to fight back the words that were coming into his mind, but he couldn't stop them. 'My dad . . . once he was the most wonderful person in the world. But he's not any more . . . I hate him!'

'Oh, Melv, I forgot . . . sorry . . .' Cas laid a hand on Melvin's arm.

Melvin found he was fighting back tears. 'Is it wrong to hate your dad?'

'You don't hate your dad,' said Cas. 'If you did you wouldn't be upset. Hating someone is easy. You hate what your dad's done – and you still love him, I guess. That's what's hard.'

'How do you know?'

'Because I love my mum,' said Cas. 'My real mum, but I hate what she did, when she gave me away.'

'But you don't know *why* she did that,' said Melvin.

'No, I don't. Not yet. And you don't know why your dad left.'

'No,' said Melvin, sadly. 'I don't. My mum's never told us.'

'Anyway, I think it's a very nice scar,' said Cas, with a smile, taking her hand away from Melvin's arm.

So intently had Melvin and Cas been wrapped up in each other's words that neither of them had heard the not altogether gentle footsteps approaching them from the drive. So it was with a sickening shock that they heard a voice behind them growl:

'Melvin Perkins and Cassandra Washbone. You two are dead meat!'

X

He paces anxiously up and down the staff room; glances at his watch. Morning school has finished. The children have gone home for the afternoon. Staff are getting ready to go up to Hogman's Thorn House for their In-Service Training course.

Esther comes in. 'No sign of the missing children?'

He shakes his head.

'It worries me, Guy,' says Esther.

'Oh, I'm sure they'll be found safe and sound.' He tries to sound reassuring.

'It's not that. I've just checked with County Hall. Their absences count as truancy. It will do the chances of us securing top place in the school league tables no good at all, I'm afraid.'

'Excuse me,' says Guy. He strides out of the staff room and down the corridor to the school office.

'You again, Mr Gibbons?' asks the school secretary, a puzzled smile on her face.

'Are you sure that no one has called at the school for me?'

'No one, Mr Gibbons.'

'And there have been no telephone calls?'

'None, Mr Gibbons.'

He shakes his head and wanders off back down

the corridor.

'Mr Gibbons, might I have a word?'

He turns and sees the new temporary school care-taker – their deadhead school caretaker – beckoning him from the doorway of his tiny cubby hole.

He goes over to him. Inside the cubby hole he can see buckets, brooms, polish, toilet rolls, great plastic cans full of disinfectant – all the items that go to make the efficient caretaking of a busy school.

He follows the caretaker in.

10

'No, Perkins! Run! It's a trap!'

'Kayleigh!' Melvin and Cas spun round and spoke together.

Kayleigh Foster smiled her brightest smile. 'If it's not Smallham's missing young lovers!'

'Shut it, Foster,' warned Cas, 'or else you'll be feeling the wrong end of your baseball bat on top of your ugly head.'

'What are you doing up here?' snapped Melvin.

'Helping my friend with his History project,' said Kayleigh. 'Where's he gone?'

From out of the undergrowth crawled Pravi. He stood up, brushed himself down and grinned at Melvin sheepishly.

'It's our lucky day, eh, Perkins?' grinned Kayleigh. She turned to Cas. 'Wait till we tell the police we've found you two. We could get a reward! Come on, Pravi, let's go and collect the cash!' Kayleigh was grinning from ear to ear.

'Foster, come back here!' called Cas in desperation, but Kayleigh had already disappeared out of the gate.

Cas grabbed Pravi's arm, anxiously. 'You haven't seen my brother – or Melv's sister, have you?' she asked anxiously.

Pravi shook his head. 'No, why? They haven't gone missing too, have they? What is it with you Washbones and Perkinses?'

'It's not funny, Pravi,' said Cas quietly.

Melvin turned to his friend. 'The deadheaders are back,' he said.

The glint went out of Pravi's eye. 'Seriously?'

'Very seriously,' said Cas.

'What do you want me to do?' Pravi asked.

'Get down to the school and tell the Gibbon to get up here right away.'

'The Gibbon?'

'Yes. Look there's no time to explain, just tell him – "they've found the attic",' said Melvin.

'Right,' said Pravi, determinedly.

'Oh, and stop Kayleigh blabbing to my mum,' added Cas.

'I'll try,' said Pravi, without conviction. He crashed his way through the branches and was gone.

'Kayleigh won't really grass us up, will she?' frowned Melvin.

Cas shook her head. 'She knows that if she did, I'd soon tell her dad she was up here snogging Pravi Patel.'

They sat down against the wall and waited for the Gibbon.

It was about half an hour later that they heard the throb of a diesel engine climbing Hogman's Hill. It came close, then stopped. From the bushes, Melvin could just see the Gibbon unlocking the gate. He rushed out, Cas followed close behind.

'Mr Gibbons!'

The Gibbon turned round. 'Did Pravi find you?'

'Yes . . .'

'We've found the evidence that proves that Obadiah Burke was a murderer!' yelled Melvin, excitedly.

'Have you seen Bunny and Hannah?' asked Cas.

The Gibbon looked distracted. 'No . . . no.'

'Then the deadhead guards must still have them!'

'I'd better take you two up to the House,' said the Gibbon, holding open the door of the school minibus.

They pulled up at the front door. 'Come on,' said the Gibbon. 'Let's go in.'

'But what about the guards?' frowned Cas.

'They'll do whatever I tell them,' said the Gibbon.

Cas followed the Gibbon in.

Melvin was just a few steps behind her when he saw Arnold flitting in front of him. 'No, Perkins! Run! It's a trap! He's a deadheader!'

'Cas!' yelled Melvin, but already he could see one of the guards had got her arms in a grip and the other guard was on his way out to get him.

Melvin sprinted round the front of the house. Any instinct to run away quickly vanished. Melvin knew he had to get inside the House. Along the front of the House he raced, then round the corner to the back – and the bottom of the fire escape. Up he clambered, his mind on one thing only, to get into the House. Half way up, he felt the ladder judder: the guard was already on the bottom rung. As he climbed, Melvin saw little showers of brick dust floating down from the sides of the ladder and with a sickening gulp he realised it was slowly coming away from the wall.

With a frantic final effort he scrambled over the parapet. Even as he did so, the fire escape swung away from the wall and crashed to the ground below. There was a yell of terror from the deadhead guard, then silence.

Melvin scampered across the roof to the skylight. He hauled it open and dropped noiselessly onto the mattress that was still on the floor of the attic below. Once his eyes had adjusted to the darkness, he saw a narrow shaft of light in the floor at the far end. This must have been the trap door the guards had climbed through in their pursuit of Bunny and Hannah. He inched his way over. Below he could just make out the hard outlines of some sort of scientific equipment . . .

'There's all the carving knives and skewers I told you about.' Arnold had appeared at Melvin's shoulder. 'Push the trap full open and drop down. No one is there.'

Keen to get into the House proper to find Cas, Melvin followed his ghost-friend's advice. As soon as he dropped to the floor, Melvin could see exactly what the room was for. What Arnold had thought of as skewers were, in fact, scalpels. What Arnold had called carving knives, were surgical knives. This was an operating theatre. This was the room where the final, grisly stage of deadheading was going to take place. This is where the deadheads' faces would be changed forever.

Melvin made his way to the door, turned the handle and pulled slowly. The door did not move. It was locked. He looked up at the trap door hole. There was no way of reaching it.

'Arnold!' he hissed in sheer panic. 'You didn't tell me the door was locked!'

But Arnold had gone.

Melvin slumped on the floor. He guessed that the next deadhead victims, the staff of Sir Norman Burke Middle School, would soon be arriving.

He didn't hear the key turn in the lock. But he saw the door opening. He stumbled to his feet and found himself staring at Cas's frightened face. Still holding her arm in a lock was the Gibbon.

'Ah, Melvin! You've found your own way here! How convenient!'

'I told you before, no one deadheads me, Mr Gibbons,' muttered Melvin, defiantly.

'Wrong on both counts,' growled Cas's captor, as with his free hand he pulled hard at his hair. Gradually the mask slid snake-like up and over his face to reveal the suntanned, smirking features of Darius O'Fee.

'Back!' he ordered Melvin. 'I'm nearer the knives

than you are.'

It happened so quickly.

Melvin stepped back. Behind him was a large free-standing operating theatre lamp. There was a switch on its arm. With a quick flick of his fist, Melvin knocked the switch on. A great beam of light filled the room, shining directly into Darius O'Fee's eyes. Instinctively, he threw his arm to shield his eyes. While he was off balance, Cas kicked out at his shins. Darius winced, and for a second his grip relaxed – ever so slightly, but enough for Cas to pull free. Darius lurched at her, but already Cas had pulled Kayleigh's baseball bat from her jacket. She swung it back, intending to aim a blow at Darius, but the operating theatre light was behind her and the bat smashed furiously into the glass. There was a dull bang. The light went out. Sparks flew and jumped and smoke started to drift out along the wires.

'The door's still locked,' yelled Cas.

Out of the corner of his eye, Melvin saw Darius pick the longest and shiniest surgical knife.

And then the door burst open.

'Don't even think about it, Darius,' shouted the Gibbon. This time it *was* the Gibbon, not one of the others in a mask, Melvin knew. That voice: it was the one he used at school when he found members of 8GG skulking in the corridor instead of being outside at breaktime.

'Cassandra, Melvin, get the blazes out of here!'

115

Down the stairs flew Cas and Melvin. Straight out of the front door and into the glare of a searchlight.

Melvin blinked. The air was filled with flashing blue lights. Officers in flak jackets charged into Hogman's Thorn House. Kayleigh had been true to her word: she had called the police.

Then Melvin noticed other flashing lights: cameras. Excited reporters with microphones surged forward. The radio, television and newspapers were here in force, too.

Detective Inspector Jinks rushed up to Melvin and Cas. 'Are you two okay?'

'Look,' said Cas, 'I've got a brown belt in judo and I've got this.' She waved Kayleigh's baseball bat close enough to Detective Inspector Jinks' face for him to have to take a step back. 'Do you think I can't handle myself?'

'Let me through! I'm his sister!' Melvin heard a shrill voice call.

Hannah came up and hugged him. The cameras popped again. Then Bunny stumbled through the crowd. More hugging. More camera popping.

'How did you get away?' asked Cas, suddenly tearful.

'It's called running for it,' said Bunny. 'As soon as we heard those guards getting the stepladder we were on that roof and down the ladder before you could say "Smallham-Kids-In-Young-Love-Runaway-Rescue-Drama". Then we contacted all the press. We thought, if light has got to be

116

shed on the darkness, then newspapers, radio and television are a pretty good way of doing it.'

Melvin looked around at the sea of eager, pleading faces and felt his mouth go dry.

'Melvin! Cas! What made you run away? Was it your dad, Melvin? Was it love, Cas?' The journalists clamoured round.

'I'll get you out of here,' said Detective Inspector Jinks, catching Melvin's panicky look.

Yes, please, thought Melvin. Perkins' First Law of Survival (Keep Your Head Down) spun round and round in his head. Then, out of the corner of his eye, he caught sight of a slight, pale figure in a ragged shirt.

He summoned the power within him. 'I'd like to say something first,' he told the startled inspector. 'To everybody here.'

Melvin looked at the mass of cameras and fluffy boom mikes. 'Cas and me are . . .' The journalists stood with bated breath. 'Are pupils at Sir Norman Burke School. Now everyone thinks that Sir Norman Burke and his father Obadiah were great and good people. But it is a lie. They ran their school here – Flogmore Hall – in the most evil way. They even murdered one of their pupils, Arnold Thomas. This is the truth. You will find the evidence in the Ice House in the far corner of the garden.'

Melvin paused. Directly in front of him stood Arnold. He was shouting something to Melvin, but he couldn't hear what it was.

117

Then Melvin saw that everybody, journalists and police, were looking not at him, but beyond him. He turned round. And saw what they were looking at.

Fanned by the ferocious wind, smoke and flames were pouring out of the upstairs windows of Hogman's Thorn House. The fire started by Cas when she had short-circuited the operating theatre lamp, had spread. The flak-jacketed police officers raced out of the house, but of Darius and the Gibbon there was no sign.

Melvin and Cas caught sight of a familiar figure pushing her way through the police cordon.

'Cassandra! What the devil have you been up to?' Councillor Mrs Washbone's voice could be heard quite distinctly above the wail of sirens and the roar of pumps. With a rueful glance at Melvin, Cas went over to her.

Then Melvin felt a familiar arm round his shoulder.

'Mum – '

'Later, Melvin,' said Mrs Perkins. Her eyes followed the searchlight's beam, which had settled on the roof, just where the fire escape ladder had been. Two figures perched there precariously, seemingly engaged in a roof-top wrestling match: Darius O'Fee and the Gibbon. There was a gasp as Darius almost succeeded in pushing the Gibbon off the roof. Already smoke was billowing from the skylight. Darius saw it and started screaming.

'Get your turntable round there!' yelled Detective Inspector Jinks.

'We can't!' the fire officer shouted. 'Too many trees and bushes!'

'Then those two are going to burn alive!'

'We'll get the safety blanket over there!'

Darius jumped first, of course, and was hauled away into the back of an ambulance. Then the Gibbon jumped. He refused to be taken away to an ambulance. He rushed across to join Cas and Melvin.

There was a thunderous crash and great sparks raced up into the sky. The Gibbon, Melvin and his mum watched as the roof which the Gibbon had been standing on only a minute before finally caved in.

'Oh, Guy,' said Mrs Perkins, laying a hand on his arm.

Melvin looked from his form tutor to his mum.

'Come on, Melvin,' said Mrs Perkins. 'We need to talk.'

They marched through the fire fighters and police officers, through the huddle of Sir Norman Burke teachers who wondered just what kind of in-service training course they had got themselves on.

They stared at Melvin as if he was some kind of weirdo. None of them knew, or would ever know, the part Melvin Perkins had played in preventing them all from becoming deadheads.

XI

They stop on the drive. Although the cars windows are of darkened glass, they can see the waiting police and journalists, not to mention the fire, quite clearly.

He turns to the driver. 'I don't know what kind of game you are playing, Miss Allbright, but you will drive me back to London, now.'

Angie Allbright does not argue.

She has seen the holster strapped across his shoulder.

Detective Inspector Jinks opens the ambulance doors. 'Right, Mr O'Fee, you've got some questions to answer.'

But Darius O'Fee is nowhere to be seen.

11

'Why haven't you told me this before, Mum?'

Melvin and his mum sat at the kitchen table.

'Guy's told me,' she said.

'Told you what?' asked Melvin.

'Told me enough,' his mum replied cryptically. 'Enough for me to know that he is a good man. Enough for me to know that I have an extraordinary son.'

Melvin knew that he would have to make do with that, by way of explanation. The rest would be buried wherever it was his mum buried her other secrets.

'I did wonder . . . when you first started going up to Hogman's Thorn,' his mum suddenly said.

'Wondered what?'

'If you knew of your connection with the place.'

Melvin's heart missed a beat. He shook his head. 'Tell me, Mum. I'm not related to the Burke dynasty, am I?'

Mrs Perkins laughed. 'Goodness gracious no! No, it's simply that you were *born* at Hogman's Thorn.'

Melvin's jaw dropped. 'Born there? But how . . . ?' he managed to stammer.

'It's like this. After old Mrs Allbright died the place was derelict for a few years.'

'Yes, I know.'

'It became a popular place for Smallham people to go to – for walks and the like. The birds you could hear in those gardens. And the trees – particularly in autumn. Which is why your dad and I were up there a fortnight before you were due. Hannah was with your gran and we thought we'd have a peaceful stroll in the grounds of the old house. Then you decided to arrive. Some other people up there drove down to Smallham and called the ambulance. It arrived just in time for you to be born in the back.'

'Why haven't you told me this before, Mum?'

'You knew you were born in the back of an ambulance.'

'Yes, but I didn't know *where.*'

'Surely we must have mentioned it at some time?'

'No.' Melvin shrugged. What other things were there that his mum thought 'we must have mentioned at some time'? As if she knew what he was thinking, Mrs Perkins reached up and took down an old vase that stood on top of the wall units. She took out a letter and handed it to Melvin.

'I should have shown it to you before,' she said quietly, 'but I always tried to forget about it. I've always *meant* to show you – if I hadn't I would've thrown it away by now.'

There was one word only on the envelope – KATE. But that one word was enough for Melvin to recognise the handwriting.

They walked over the charred remains of Hogman's

Thorn House. The fire had taken some of the trees close to the garden, so that the whole garden was now much lighter than it had been before.

As they approached the dark side of the grounds, Melvin realised that it was different. It didn't *feel* so dark or so menacing. Now that the house itself was gone you could still see the light side of the grounds. You weren't surrounded by the shadows.

They sat down among the burnt-out furniture and timbers of the old house.

'What did the letter from your dad say?' asked Cas.

Melvin shrugged. 'Just that he'd found someone else. And that he was making a clean break.'

'And that was all?'

'That was all,' said Melvin, quietly. 'It doesn't make it hurt any the less, but in a way I feel better about it all because I know the truth.'

Cas frowned. 'How do you mean?'

'Like I used to imagine that Dad had left because he was working on a secret mission for the Army or he'd gone off to build a house with a swimming pool for us in America somewhere. It hurt knowing he'd left; but it also hurt not knowing why he'd left.'

They sat in silence for a moment. 'Arnold's gone too, hasn't he?' whispered Cas.

Melvin nodded. 'At least, if he is still around, I can't see him anymore. Letting everyone know the truth about his death and destroying the evil of the Burke dynasty really did avenge his murder.'

'Now, he can rest in peace, as they say,'

123

nodded Cas.

'I suppose so. A bit like my memories of my dad.'

'Will you miss Arnold?'

Melvin thought. 'I don't know. He was already getting a bit of a strain.'

'How do you mean?'

'He never changed. He was still the same as when I first saw him last summer.'

'You've changed, Melvin.'

'Perhaps . . .'

He took her hand as they walked back down the drive towards the road.

'. . . I certainly wouldn't have been walking down here holding your hand like this a year ago,' he added.

'You bet you wouldn't. I would have thumped your head in good and proper,' replied Cas, indignantly. She squeezed his hand. 'It's the end of the Burke Dynasty – the end of deadheading, isn't it?' asked Cas.

'It is,' Melvin nodded.

'Guy's still around, of course,' added Cas.

'You're telling me he's around,' chuckled Melvin. 'He's taking mum out to dinner *again* tonight.'

'He's a good 'un,' said Cas. 'For a teacher, at any rate.'

'Yes,' Melvin agreed. 'He comes from the light side of the house, that's what Arnold said. Like me, I suppose. Darius, Harry and Angie were all born on the dark side.'

'I wonder how long it will be before he marries your mum,' said Cas airily.

'The Gibbon?' asked Melvin incredulously.

'I don't mean Darius or Harry now, do I?'

'My mum isn't going to marry the Gibbon!'

'Of course she is!' retorted Cas. 'Look, Melvin Perkins, you may have special powers and be ultra-sensitive to paranormal beings and what-not, but when it comes to intuition about people, I am top of the Super League.'

'Cas – '

'Who sorted out your sister and my brother?'

'Who thought Esther was a deadhead?' responded Melvin.

'So did you,' said Cas.

'Anyone could make that mistake,' said Melvin. 'Mind you, you *were* right about Kayleigh. You said her baseball bat might save my life. And it did! Yes, Cas, when it comes to baseball bats you really know what you're talking about. But with anything else – aaargh!'

Melvin suddenly found himself flat on his back on the grass verge, looking up at the sky.

'I'm also a judo brown belt, fish-face.'

Cas charged off down Hogman's Hill. Melvin scrambled to his feet and raced after her. He caught her up and took her hand again. Then all the way down into Smallham they called each other silly names and laughed, like the old, true friends they had become.

XII

They know it can never work now. Obadiah Burke's dark secrets are public knowledge. The Black Book is available in the County Library store for any scholar to borrow. The House has gone. And with it their power.

Guy has sold the farm, which was his alone to sell.

Harry Summerskill is now employed as a marketing director by a multi-national conglomerate, specialising in soft drinks and industrial cleaning fluids.

Angie Allbright now works as a Public Relations consultant for a particularly thuggish Near Eastern dictator.

Darius O'Fee is one of the most popular preachers – and fund raisers – on American television.

None of them is known by these names, of course.

Keen to make whatever money they could from their failed deadheading venture, they all sold their share of Hogman's Thorn House to Guy.

No new house will ever be built at Hogman's Thorn. It is now a Wildlife Park.

Sir Norman Burke Middle School is now simply Smallham Middle School.

Kayleigh can't understand how she ever fancied that 'drip Melvin Perkins' – at least that's what she tells her new boyfriend, Pravi Patel.

Hannah is still a fruitarian, except when Bunny is cooking her burger and chips at his flat in Brighton.

Guy is still taking Melvin's mum out.

And Arnold Thomas, as Melvin rightly surmised, now rests in eternal peace.